STOOL PIGEON

"Louis Malley obviously knew how the mob and the cops operated in his era. He uses that knowledge and creates some fine character studies in this suspenseful, fast-paced novel. Every page of *Stool Pigeon* feels real and true."
—Elgin Bleecker, *The Dark Time*

"Malley's creates a bleak, dirty and depressed setting for the streets of Little Italy in the early 50's. He does it so well, the reader wishes for snow to come to clean the place up. This is an excellent novel."
—*Vintage Hardboiled Reads*

HORNS OF THE DEVIL

"*Horns for the Devil* is an honest tale that portrays mafiosos as truthful and real as De Niro's A Bronx Tale. Loved every word of it."—*GoodReads*

"This shows how the 'Organization' takes hold of one second generation Sicilian at birth, and never relaxes its hold throughout his short life in New York's lower East Side slums.... Sensational material."
—*Kirkus Reviews*

Louis Malley Bibliography

Horns for the Devil (1951; reissued as
   Shadow of the Mafia, 1958)
Stool Pigeon (1953; reissued as
   Shakedown Strip, 1960)
Tiger in the Street (1957)
The Love Mill (1961)

STOOL PIGEON
Louis Malley

Black Gat Books • Eureka California

STOOL PIGEON

Published by Black Gat Books
A division of Stark House Press
1315 H Street
Eureka, CA 95501, USA
griffinskye3@sbcglobal.net
www.starkhousepress.com

STOOL PIGEON
Originally published 1953 in paperback by Avon
Books, New York, and copyright © 1953 by Louis
Malley. Reprinted 1960 by Avon Books as Shakedown
Strip.

ISBN-13: 978-1-944520-81-6

Book design by Mark Shepard, SHEPGRAPHICS.COM
Cover art by James Meese from the 1953 edition of
Stool Pigeon.
Proofreading by Bill Kelly

First Stark House Press/Black Gat Edition:
August 2019

PART ONE

He walked around the car and studied it carefully. When he came to the open door he looked in. The clock in the fancy dashboard said six. The radio was on and a happy voice said, "Good Morning," while an organ played Christmas music.

The car's engine was still running. He leaned over and turned it off. Then he saw the cigar burning black bubbles in the rubber floor-mat. He took a pencil from his pocket and pressed the cigar out. When he was finished he wiped the pencil off and put it back in his pocket.

Then he looked at Tony Statella. Tony seemed comfortable behind the wheel. The only thing wrong was the big hole in Tony's head, where the bullet had plowed out and splattered blood and brains over the seat.

He could see tomorrow's headlines. Big, black and loud. One newspaper was running a daily box, like a baseball score. He sighed. Tony's death would make it read seventeen killed in twenty-one days—and no arrests.

So far Manhattan had been quiet. But now Tony had to take a bullet right here in Little Italy. The peace was over. The papers, the mayor's office and the Department—they would all be crawling on his back.

Well, he was getting tired. If they pushed too hard he'd tell them where they could stick his badge.

The happy voice on the radio was explaining that no woman could be content on Christmas Day without a bottle of perfume. There was no use letting the battery run down. He switched the radio off and backed out of the car, making sure he didn't touch anything else.

"Got his Christmas present a day early, huh?"

He turned and looked at the young cop.

"You the first one here?"

"Yeah," The cop said. "I was around the block checking doors and heard the shot. When I got here I saw the blonde dame." The cop pointed to a girl sitting on the stairs in front of a tenement house. "The dame was half in the car. She stayed like that until I asked her if she was hurt. Then she started to scream. What a set of pipes!" The cop rubbed his red ears. "She finally stopped. I figure she was getting into the car when someone came around the driver's side, poked a gun at the guy's head and pulled the trigger."

"What else did you see?"

"That big fellow over there."

The cop pointed to a man standing alone near the street light. The collar on the man's camel-hair coat was up and he couldn't see the face. But there was something familiar about the broad-shouldered figure.

"What about the guy?"

"He was coming up those stairs from the cellar." The cop said. "It's a high-class Italian restaurant down there. They're open all night and they serve drinks after legal hours. Every couple of weeks I put it on my report." The cop shrugged. "But no one closes it up."

"Then what happened?"

"In a few seconds the squad car came. Then a load of men from Division. Then you fellows from Homicide."

"And that's all?"

"Yeah." The cop said. "You may not know it, but this is an Italian neighborhood. Mostly respectable and dead as hell."

He knew the neighborhood. He turned away from the cop and looked down the dreary morning street.

A couple of bums had drifted across from the Bowery to take in the excitement. Two garbage men were asking a detective from Division when they could pick up the garbage. Across the street the chef and the night man stood in front of the coffee pot and watched.

He knew the neighborhood. He'd been born in one of the tenements a block away. He had chalked kick-me-hard on the sidewalk and played kick-the-can in the street. He'd met girls on the roofs and rolled dice in the cellars. And on Saturdays he'd washed celery and trimmed lettuce in the vegetable store across the way.

Now the street was cluttered with police cars and a dead man. And he, Detective Vincent Milazzo of Homicide, was in charge of the whole production. Local boy makes good. Better he should be home sleeping.

He took the pipe from his pocket and turned away from the raw morning wind to light it.

"This is my first murder," the cop said. "It's exciting."

But the young cop was the only one getting any kicks. The laboratory men worked around the car complaining about the cold. The police photographer was taking his pictures as fast as he could and the boys from the morgue huddled in a doorway and waited for the dead man.

Man! Tony Statella—procurer, narcotics peddler, and rapist. He wasn't a man. Better to save everyone the trouble and drop the stiff into a sewer. He sighed. The sewer would probably vomit.

Well, tomorrow would be a better Christmas Day without Tony around. But that wasn't the point. The badge in his pocket said he had to go through the motions of trying to find the killer.

He started over to the blonde. She was sitting on the stairs alongside some fancy Christmas packages. The bottom of her mink coat was on the sidewalk and she was crying like a baby into a pair of smooth white hands. Each finger was tipped with a long gold-colored nail.

When he got closer he saw the drying spots where Tony's blood had splashed all over her. He called one of the boys from Homicide.

"Take her home," he said. "Let her change her clothes. Then get her back. And see she doesn't talk to anyone."

He watched them walk her to the police car. Maybe she was twenty. Maybe without the mink and the paint and the peroxide she was only sixteen. A cop put the Christmas packages on the seat next to her, slammed the door and the car took off.

That left the big guy in the camel-hair coat. As he walked toward him he suddenly recognized the straight nose and the hard jaw. Rocky Tosco. He bit into the stem of his pipe and smiled. The dull feeling of routine was gone. Maybe this was it. Maybe all the years of waiting were over.

Rocky was grinning at him.

"So it's my old buddy, Detective First-Grade Vincent Milazzo."

"That's right, Rocky. What happened?"

"I was locking my restaurant," Rocky said. "Then I heard the shot. By the time I got up the stairs all I see is the babe looking in the car. Then the cop came."

"The word," he took the pipe from his mouth, "is policeman."

"Sorry," Rocky shrugged his heavy shoulders. "Policeman. Then the babe starts to scream. I don't know what scared her more, the killing or the cop. Excuse me." Rocky smiled. "I mean policeman."

Still the same old cocky Rocky.

"You got more questions, Detective Milazzo?"

"Plenty."

"Then how about going down to my restaurant where it's warm."

He looked around the street. The stiff was being shoved into the meat wagon. The boys from the lab were finishing up on the car. The garbage had been picked up. And when people stopped for a look the young cop kept them moving.

There was no need to hang around and freeze. He pointed to the restaurant and followed Rocky down the stairs. Rocky opened the door and turned on the lights.

There was red wall paper with white zebras. Plenty of fresh flowers and a stainless steel kitchen behind a plate glass window.

He sat down at one of the tables and flipped a menu over. Veal and peppers was three fifty. A plate of spaghetti was two and a half. Some joint—he could just about scrape together the price of a demitasse and a tip.

The black leather bar was covered with ashtrays and half-filled glasses. There was enough evidence of drinks being sold after the legal hour to pepper the joint and salt Rocky away for a long time.

But he was from Homicide. He was just supposed to find killers. A liquor violation wasn't his department. Rocky knew it too because Rocky stood there smiling at him. That same smile. How many times had he promised himself to kick it off Rocky's face. Who could tell? This might be his chance.

He watched Rocky get out of his camel-hair coat and lay it over the back of a chair. Rocky's nutria-colored gabardine suit with the hand stitching made him remember he ought to get his other suit out of the cleaners for the Holidays.

Rocky's soft-looking, highly polished shoes made him stick his own under the table. Sometime next week he'd buy another pair.

And Rocky's tie, pulled together in a small hard knot, made him think of his own tie. He got it last Christmas from an aunt. But he didn't have to worry about buying a new tie. Tomorrow his aunt would give him three more.

What the hell—he was better-looking than Rocky, just as tall and twice as smart. Why was he feeling sorry for himself? Could he be jealous of the punk? Jealous of Rocky's barbershop sunburn? The manicured nails and fancy clothes?

No use kidding himself—he was jealous, so jealous it made him sick. How he'd love to pin this murder on Rocky Tosco.

"What was Tony Statella doing here at six in the morning?"

Rocky leaned back against the bar.

"That blonde dame upstairs is my hat chick. She's also Tony's regular girl. He hung around and took her home from work."

"What was Tony's racket these days?"

"You know better than me."

"Don't be bashful, Rocky."

Rocky turned his big back and started to shove an ashtray back and forth on the bar. He was taking too long to answer.

"Far as I know," Rocky finally said, "Tony was legit. He had some cigarstand concessions in hotel lobbies."

"Is that how he got the fancy car, the mink for his girl, and the big cigars?"

"He got his cigars wholesale." Rocky turned around and faced him. "Look, the guy wasn't my brother. How do you expect me to know?"

The words made sense. Yet underneath that barbershop tan and two-hundred-dollar suit Rocky was working up a sweat. Why?

He remembered Tony Statella sitting behind the wheel of his new car. That wasn't a cold killing. A professional killer would have stood in the middle of the street and pumped lead until the gun was empty. Anybody who is mad enough to hang a gun on the edge of a guy's ear in order to shake up his brains must be carrying a bad hate—a jealous woman, or maybe a crossed business partner.

He looked around the restaurant, then back to Rocky. "Did Tony own a piece of this joint?"

"I got no partners." Rocky was real proud. "The place is all mine."

"How's business?"

"No complaints."

"Most restaurant owners are crying the blues. And you have a big overhead here, too."

"My rent's cheap."

"I'm talking about your payoff, Rocky. Your protection. It costs plenty to keep this place open after legal hours. How do you get the money?"

"Instead of butter I serve oleomargarine."

He took his time lighting up his pipe. Then he started asking questions again.

"How was Tony getting on with his blonde?"

"Smooth."

"Maybe Tony had another girl."

"Tony?" Rocky laughed. "Girls hung around Tony like cops hang around apples on a pushcart."

He took the pipe out of his mouth.

"Rocky."

"Yeah."

"When you were nine—" he kept his voice soft—"I called you a crook because you marked the cards. Then you ran to your old man's butcher shop, got a cleaver and chased me off the block."

"Yeah." Rocky was laughing. "I remember."

"I walked around all that day thinking how I was going to kill you. But when I got home I found your mother crying to my mother. That saved you because my mother made me promise I wouldn't touch you. But if you make one more crack about the police—as big as you are, I'm going to beat the face off your head."

Rocky was ready to answer when the door opened. The

young cop walked in, banging his hands together. The boys from the lab followed.

And then Whiteman, his partner, came in and walked over to the table.

"Milazzo," Whiteman said. "The reporters want to ask questions."

"Let them save their time. I don't know the answers." He looked at Rocky. "Leave us alone a few minutes. I'll talk to you later."

The big punk smiled and walked down to the far end of the bar and started talking to one of the boys from the lab.

"Should I let the reporters in to warm up?" Whiteman asked.

"Keep them out."

"They won't like you for it."

"I stopped trying to make people like me a long time ago."

"You're doing a good job," Whiteman said.

He watched his partner pull out a chair and sit down.

He and Whiteman worked together pretty well, to a point. But he didn't like Whiteman. The guy had been up on graft charges. It happened only once, but you could never tell when Whiteman would slip again.

And Whiteman didn't like Italians. Not that he said it out loud, or made anything of it, but being an Italian you knew. It was a raw nerve in your head, like a tooth that doesn't hurt until the dentist splashes it with cold water. Often he said to himself, so Whiteman doesn't like Italians—so what do I care? But he did care. Every time they booked a wop or the corpse turned out to be an Italian he got the feeling Whiteman was thinking what so many other people think. Spaghetti and gangsters—that's all Italian people were good for.

Whiteman was looking at the menu and shaking his

head at the prices. He was a short, thick guy with a heavy face. He got the crooked nose one night while stopping a hopped-up purse snatcher. Whiteman was forty-five. Ten years older than he was. And he had worked eight years longer on the police force. But was still only detective second-grade. Maybe that made Whiteman sore too. Working under a guy he considered a kid.

Some kid. He was thirty-five and he felt as old as the Statue of Liberty and just as rusty.

"Well," he said to Whiteman. "What did you find upstairs?"

Whiteman pushed the menu away and leaned back. "The stiff is Tony Statella."

"Yeah. I recognized the way he used to part his hair. What about Tony?"

"At seventeen he was put away for raping a nurse. Then he picked up four narcotic charges, but only one conviction. Next he was nailed for the Mann Act. A fifteen-year-old girl and her thirteen-year-old sister. He got off with three years."

"Nice guy."

"There's more."

"I know all that. What's he been doing lately?"

"I was talking to that young guy Scotti, upstairs. He's a Division detective."

"Don't know him."

"You should. He's Italian too."

"I don't know every Italian." He was sorry he said it so loud. He lowered his voice. "What did this Division detective have to say?"

"That Tony couldn't keep away from women."

"What did he have to say about Rocky Tosco?"

"He said Rocky was clean."

He jerked the pipe out of his mouth and came forward in the chair.

"Detective Scotti is a liar."

"I don't know," Whiteman said. "The guy's got a reputation for being a straight cop."

"Stop conning me, Whiteman. What kind of a place is this?"

Whiteman turned to look at the bar and the sticky, half-filled glasses.

"It's an after-hour joint."

"Sure. You know, and I know. The cop on the beat turns it in on his report every week. Yet the police never dose the place. Why?"

His partner shrugged.

"Come on, Whiteman, say it. What department is supposed to make the pinch?"

"Division."

"That's right. Detective Scotti. The guy who comes running around to tell us Rocky is clean. Your friend Scotti is a liar and a crook."

Whiteman leaned over and touched his coat sleeve.

"Easy, Vincent. Think what you want to, but don't talk—not unless you're ready to get hurt."

Whiteman was right. He pushed his pipe into his mouth and sat back. Murder was his business. And that was trouble enough without stepping on Division's toes. He tried lighting his pipe but it wouldn't take. He dug the old tobacco out with his pencil and filled the pipe again. By the time he had it going he was cooled off.

"Well, Whiteman, what do you know about Rocky?"

"If I say not much you'll jump me. But it's true. His old man was pulled out of Long Island Sound with a pair of cement shoes. One brother was a big-shot in the thirties. Public Enemy Number Seven. Sent up for manslaughter. Broke jail and ran wild. They finally killed him in a farmhouse. The younger brother is clean. He works for the Post Office."

"And Rocky?"

"You know all this stuff better than anyone. Why do you keep pumping?"

"Something may have slipped my mind."

"Nothing ever slips your mind. It's like a filing cabinet. Rocky Tosco." Whiteman thought a minute. "About a month after he got out of the Navy he was arrested for armed robbery. Gasoline station. No conviction. Three years ago he bought this joint. Then it was a hole in the floor. Now it's big-time. He draws a crowd of entertainers from the Village night clubs. They come here after the last show is over. That brings in the playboys and the hot rocks who like chorus girls."

"How did he do it, Whiteman? From nothing to big-shot in three years. The joint is worth at least fifty grand. The payoff to keep it open must be at least a thousand a week. Who does Rocky pay?"

"I don't know."

"I don't either. But I bet our friend Detective Scotti from Division gets a piece of it."

"You may be wrong about Scotti. The kid has done a lot of good police work the last few years. He's gone up quick and honest. A lot like you."

"Italian?"

"No. I mean he's all cop. A natural, who loves it. And he's got a good name." Whiteman's voice went low. "You don't get a good name easy in this business."

He had to look away from Whiteman. He knew what his partner was getting at. A few years ago Whiteman had been on top. Then a Brooklyn bookie picked him and thirty-four other cops out of a line-up. The charge was accepting a bribe. They broke Whiteman down to the sidewalk. Now he was coming up again. But with a black mark against his name it was slow and hard.

"What else did you find upstairs?"

"The fellow in the coffee pot heard the shot but that's all."

"What about the two bums?"

"They didn't see a thing."

"For a cigarette they'd kill the President."

"Are you kidding? They're so soaked in wine they can't find the zipper on their pants, let alone a trigger."

"Was there anything in the car?"

"Yeah. This." Whiteman pulled something out of his pocket and tossed it on the table. "I found it in the glove compartment."

It was a small pack of photos held together with a rubber band. The picture on top was a pretty girl in a pretty dress. He rolled the rubber band off and looked at the next picture. Same girl but no dress. The third picture showed the girl stepping out of her slip. By the time he got to the twelfth picture the girl had nothing on but a wink. He went through the rest of the pile. All duplicates. Five sets of the same pictures.

"What do you make of it?"

"Nothing," Whiteman said. "Every school kid has a set or two hidden away."

"But five of the same set?"

"Maybe Tony gave them to friends."

He looked at the girl's face. A young, pretty kid. He wondered what made them do things like that.

"What did the lab boys find?"

"What they always find. Nothing." Then Whiteman leaned forward. "Vince. Do yourself a favor. Let those reporters in."

He knew Whiteman was right. If he didn't let them in there would be hell to pay. They'd start burning the wires with complaints. Then he'd get a lecture on freedom of the press and good public relations. And if he let them in they would blast him and the whole police department in tomorrow's papers anyway.

"Hey, Rocky," he called and Rocky came over from the other end of the bar. "You got a private office where I can talk to you?"

Rocky pointed to a side door.

"Okay, Whiteman, let them in. But keep them away from me."

He followed Rocky into the office.

It was a small room with a leather couch, two chairs and a desk. He walked behind the desk and sat down. Over in the corner near a filing cabinet he saw a couple of cardboard boxes neatly tied with rope, and he wondered what was inside. Then he looked at the drinking glass on the table. It was holding a couple of plain, ordinary six-inch spikes.

Rocky saw him looking at them and laughed.

"I'll show you," Rocky said.

He took a spike out of the glass and held it up. Then slowly and easily he twisted it with his heavy fingers into a circle.

"That's nothing," Rocky said.

He kept twisting until the spike was a neat figure eight. Then he laid it down on the desk.

"Watch this." Rocky slipped out of his jacket and held his hand out straight. He rolled his fingers into a big fist and flexed his arm. The sleeve of his shirt popped and ripped into shreds.

Rocky did it to the other sleeve. Then he put both hands on his head, tensed his back and the shirt came apart to make room for the bulging muscles.

"You're wearing your shirts too small, Rocky."

"Nothing wrong with my shirts."

Rocky slipped out of the rags and walked to the mirror over the couch. He linked his fingers behind his head and watched the knots jump and dance in his arms and shoulders.

"Pretty good, huh? Look at this."

Rocky swung his back around and it was a series of long hard bumps. Then he sucked in his stomach and it knotted up like a bunch of cables. There wasn't a soft spot on the guy's body. And he was big.

"So what are you selling, Rocky?"

"Me, Milazzo. I'm telling you I spend four hours a day in the gym. I don't drink. I don't smoke." He made a big hard fist. "I could kill a man with one punch."

"So?"

"Lay off me, Milazzo. Just because a guy stopped a bullet outside my restaurant, don't try to mess me up. I won't let you shove me."

"Why are you so scared, Rocky?"

"Who's scared?"

"You. You're trying too hard for a guy who's innocent."

"I'll tell you why, Milazzo. I got a neat setup here. And I don't want any trouble. But you're out to get me. All your life you've been jealous of me."

"Jealous of you?" He tried to laugh.

"Yeah. Ever since we were kids. Then later on with Gina."

"Gina?"

He had to light his pipe again to hide his face. He couldn't help it. The name, especially coming from Rocky's thick lips, made him turn white.

"What Gina are you talking about, Rocky?"

"Gina Rossi."

He leaned back and blew some smoke out of his mouth.

"Oh, yeah," he said. "Gina Rossi. Nice kid."

"You're not fooling me, Detective." Rocky looked at himself in the mirror once more and then he turned around and laughed. "You was nuts about Gina."

Rocky went to the filing cabinet. He stepped around

the two cardboard boxes and pulled a drawer out. The drawer was full of shirts. Rocky picked one to match his suit and started putting it on.

"Yeah, Milazzo. Everybody said you was the best-looking guy on the block. You got a good build, and Gina was nuts about you. But I got her." Rocky smiled. "And I kept her until I was finished."

After all these years he didn't think it could still hurt so much. He didn't think it could still make him want to kill Rocky so bad, to get up and hit that cocky smile, to bang at the face until it was as raw as a piece of bloody liver.

"You're right about one thing, Rocky." He made himself talk low and slow. "I don't like you. I have lots of things not to like you for. And you can pop your muscles all over the joint. It's not going to stop me. When the time comes I'll get you. And you'll be soft. Soft and squashy like a stepped-on banana. Now get out and send White-man in."

Rocky took his time putting on his tie and jacket. He looked once more in the mirror and evened up the points on his breast-pocket handkerchief. Then, still smiling, he walked out.

He stared at Rocky's shredded shirt lying on the couch. Then suddenly he leaned over and picked up the spike. When they were kids he could always beat Rocky up. And now, even though the big punk spent four hours a day in the gym, Rocky didn't scare him. But that spike was really bent. He was still trying to pull it straight when his partner opened the door.

"The girl's back," Whiteman said.

He tossed the spike into the wastebasket.

"Send her in."

While he waited he remembered the brown cardboard boxes near the filing cabinet. He got up and as he started toward them the door opened and the girl came in. She was wearing a white sport coat, a pair of black slacks and a black turtle-neck sweater. There wasn't much paint on her face now and her eyes were as red as a couple of stop lights.

"Sit down." He pointed to a chair. Then he bent over and started pulling at the rope on one of the packages. He finally got a corner of the top pulled back and slipped some stuff out. Pictures. Glossy photos.

He pulled out more. There were hundreds in the box. No, thousands. All sets of twelve. All girls climbing out of their clothes. He pushed most of the pictures back and dropped a few into his pocket. Then he stood up.

"I'm Detective Milazzo from Homicide," he told the girl as he walked back to the desk.

"My name is Bernadette Duprey."

He sat down and stared at her. She was a real beauty, the kind of a girl any guy would look at twice. But the name was as phony as her blonde hair, and as young as she was, he could see the little wrinkles of night life around her eyes.

It was the same old story. Mink-hungry girls who came to take the city over and caught a poison like Tony Statella. Next week it would be some other guy. From bed to bed. In a couple of years she would wind up a scabby body in the morgue.

The guy at Juvenile Court told him they were children from broken homes. But that was hearts and flowers. Look at Gina Rossi. She came from a good Italian family. The best. And she took up with that mothball Rocky.

No. It was just the way the world was going. Everything rotten, corrupt, crooked. And little tin-badge Milazzo was trying to stop it. He'd better turn in his badge and get a soft job as night watchman in a department store. Even working in his uncle's filet house at the fish market would be better. Fish couldn't smell as bad as Tony Statella or

Rocky Tosco or the future this young girl had picked for herself.

"How long did you know Tony?"

"About six months. We were engaged." She held out her finger to show a flashing square diamond. "We were going to get married. Now this happened."

She started to wipe her eyes with a handkerchief. He lit his pipe as he waited.

"Why did Rocky Tosco kill Tony?" he finally asked.

"Rocky?" The girl looked up. "Rocky didn't kill Tony."

"Then who did?"

"I don't know."

"Yeah," he said. "You were three feet away from the killing and now you're going to tell me you didn't see."

"I saw him. He was a young fellow. But I don't know him."

"Could you recognize his picture?"

"I think so."

He almost bit the stem off his pipe. But he kept the interest out of his voice.

"You ever see the fellow before?"

"Just once. Earlier in the evening. He came into the restaurant asking to see Tony. He was all upset. They showed him to Tony's table. They talked a few minutes, then the fellow left."

"Is that all?"

"Until we started home. I was getting into the car. This fellow came from nowhere. I could see him plainly. I saw the gun, heard the shot." She buried her face in her hands. "It was terrible."

So now he had a witness. A good reliable eyewitness. He should be happy. The laboratory could keep their fancy charts, the handwriting experts could stay out of court, the lawyers for the defense could twist and turn. Let them pull all their law books off the shelves looking for tricks. He had an eyewitness. What more could a cop want?

But he was sick. The dull feeling of routine had come down on him again. That and disappointment. He had wanted to pin this one on Rocky.

Cocky Rocky.

Maybe the girl was lying. Maybe she'd go through all the pictures in Central and not be able to find the fellow, because there was no such fellow. Just an idea she and Rocky got up.

"You and Rocky good friends?"

"Yes."

"How good?"

The girl looked at him.

"What do you mean?"

"You and Rocky weren't playing around behind Tony's back?"

She looked at him as if he were dirt.

"Don't get sore," he said. "I'm a detective. I got to ask all kinds of questions."

"The answer to that one is no. Rocky and I were friends. He never even tried to get fresh. He's a perfect gentleman."

He wanted to say something about that, but he just took the pipe out of his mouth and stared at it.

"How about Tony and Rocky?" he finally asked.

"They were very good friends."

"How did they get along in business?"

"Fine."

He put the pipe back in his mouth and smiled.

"Partners, weren't they?"

"Yes," the girl said.

So Rocky had lied about that; it was the first hole in Rocky's story. He had a feeling that before the day was finished there would be plenty more.

He pulled the pictures out of his pocket and spread them on the desk.

"You still posing for these?"

"No." The girl said. Then her face got red.

"Why did you stop?"

"I only did it once."

"Why?"

"That's my business."

She was right. He was from Homicide. His business was to find who planted the bullet in Tony's ear. He was supposed to rush this girl down to Central to look at pictures and hope that she could really pick the killer. Then all he had to do was make the pinch and turn it over to the District Attorney's office.

The papers would have to play it up. The box score would read seventeen murders, twenty-one days, one arrest by Detective Vincent Milazzo. Every cop in Homicide would bless him for taking the newspapers off their necks. He would be a hero.

Then why was he feeling so miserable, sitting here trying to figure out how to pin this thing on Rocky? It wasn't only the cleaver chase, the stitches in his head, or the beating he took under the bridge. That was kid stuff. It wasn't even the way his father died, anymore. Or Gina Rossi.

It was just waiting year in and year out. Waiting for Rocky Tosco to get what he deserved. But instead of justice, Rocky went on getting bigger cars, fancier clothes and a cockier smile. And a cop with a couple of cheap suits, a couple of burnt pipes, eight hundred dollars in the bank, a furnished room, and no one to talk to but a twenty-dollar radio, was waiting for justice. Waiting for Rocky to get it.

He stood up and walked over to the girl.

"What's your name? Your real name?"

The girl looked down at her hands.

"Mary." She finally said. "Mary Herchiemer."

"Where are you from, Mary?"

"Fort Wayne, Indiana."

"Why did you come to New York?"

"I met this boy at a dancehall and he told me I ought to be a model."

"So you packed up and came here cold."

"No. This boy gave me a letter to Tony."

"Yeah." He walked back and sat down behind the desk. "Who was this boy?"

"I didn't know him very well."

"Well enough to get a letter."

"It was just a note. He wrote it on the back of a card. He used to come around the hall to dance. He told me Tony could help me get a job, so I left Fort Wayne."

It had the old familiar ring. The guy was a steerer, a fancy-dressing, fast-talking punk who picked up extra change persuading young kids to make the jump. The card to Tony was a notice that a cut was due if the girl kicked in.

He looked at the diamond on the girl's finger. Well, she had done better than most, and Tony had paid off. The steerer made himself twenty-five bucks, or maybe fifty.

"What did you do in New York?"

"I looked Tony up. I told him I wanted to be a model. He said I needed a set of pictures. All models and professional people need them before they can get a job. Well, I didn't have the right clothes or the money."

"So?"

"Tony sent me to a photographer."

"Who was he?"

"I don't remember." The girl looked up at him. "Honestly, I was a stranger. I didn't know the streets. The photographer let me borrow some clothes and gave me the pictures on credit."

"But first you did some work for him."

"How did you know?"

"When you eat garlic, Mary, your breath smells. When you're a detective you know every filthy trick in the book. So you posed for a strip set."

"Just one. Later on, when Tony and I became friends, he got the negatives back and destroyed them."

"Big-hearted Tony. He decided you were good enough to keep for himself. When he finished he was going to put your pictures back in circulation."

"That's a lie." The girl stood up. "We were engaged. We were going to be married."

"Yeah. That's right. I forgot. Sit down, Mary."

She sat down.

"What else did you do in New York?"

"I worked in one of Tony's cigar stores for a week. Then he got me this job."

"What about all the other girls?"

"I don't know what you're talking about."

"The girls who came in from Detroit. And Little Oaks. And Deerfield. The girls who Tony didn't fall for. The girls whose negatives he didn't rip up. What about them, Mary? What else did they do for Tony after he had their pictures?"

The girl didn't answer.

"So you took a mink coat and tried to wrap it around your conscience. It doesn't work, Mary. Every time you put it on think of what some poor kid had to do so Tony could buy it for you."

The girl stood up again.

"You can't talk to me like that."

"Sit down, Mary. Sit down."

The girl sat down and he smoked his pipe and stared at her.

After she picked the picture of the killer he would need her statement. A nice tight statement to give the District Attorney. A statement the defense lawyers could pound away at without being able to shake a sentence loose.

Now he had to soften Mary up. Make her feel he was a friend so she would say just what he wanted. And if she was lying, and Rocky was the killer, it would still be smart to have her on his side.

"How old are you, Mary?"

"Nineteen."

"Folks living?"

"Yes."

"You send them money?"

She nodded.

"They'd be sick if they knew where that money came from."

"I don't know what you mean."

"I believe you, Mary. I honestly believe you kept it out of your mind. Tony was good to you, so you told yourself Tony was good to everybody. But deep down you knew you were lying; you knew more about Tony's business than you want to admit. You heard talk here and there. Why don't you stop kidding yourself and tell me what you know."

"You mean be a stool pigeon?"

"Some people call it being a stoolie. Some call it being a good citizen."

"I don't know a thing."

"Sure, Mary. Don't talk now. Just think about it. And when this thing is over I want you to go home to your father and mother. I want you to forget all about this mess."

The girl put her face in her hands and started to cry. She felt mixed up now and homesick. But in a day or two some playboy would flash her a smile and a bank roll and she'd be off to the stars again.

And was he any better than the playboys? Giving her a big-brother routine, getting her all weepy and soft so he could pull a statement out of her. He was using her just like the rest.

He got up, crossed the office and opened the door. It was quiet. Everyone was gone except Rocky and Whiteman. He motioned and his partner came over.

"Show her the pictures in Central," he said. "Then see what they found in Tony's room. One more thing." He pulled the photos out of his pocket. "Where would a guy buy these things?"

"More pictures?"

"Yeah."

Whiteman thought a moment.

"There's a barber near my house in the Bronx who sells them. And there's a small store on Sixth Avenue where that's all they sell."

"Good. Go to the store. Wait around for half an hour. See what's doing. See how many guys go in and buy."

"Thinking of going into the business?"

"Anything would be better than policing. When you're finished pick me up. I'll be wandering around the street seeing what I can find." He turned and looked into the office. "Mary."

The girl got up.

"Detective Whiteman is going to show you the Rogues' Gallery so you can pick out the killer's picture. In the meantime think about what I told you."

He waited until they were gone. Then he walked over to where Rocky was leaning against the bar. He spread the nude photos out in his hand like a fan and waved them in front of Rocky's face. Rocky's grin went thin.

"I'm going to build a case against you, Rocky."

"Your business is murder, Milazzo."

"Your business was the restaurant, but you expanded.

Maybe I'll expand too."

"You asking me for money, Detective?"

He flipped the pictures in Rocky's face. For a moment Rocky's grin was gone. But slowly it came back.

"In my book you're finished, Rocky."

"Your book's been wrong a long time, Detective."

Outside in the street the big round clock in front of the jeweler's said eight-thirty. People were pushing against the cold wind to get to the subway. But today they were smiling. Even the overloaded mailman said good morning to everyone who passed. All the building janitors were out hanging wreaths and bells, waiting for the tenants to come out with the yearly envelope.

Some men with ladders were stringing a big sign across the street. A red and green sign that wished everybody a Merry Christmas and a Happy New Year for the West Side Progressive Club.

A man with a newspaper cupped a hand over his mouth and hollered to another man across the street.

"Hey Sal, papers say snow for tonight."

Snow. People looked up at the cold gray sky, smiled and kept on walking.

The day before Christmas in Little Italy.

For him it was like someone slipped off the front of each tenement. He knew so well what was going on in each room. In each heart.

He remembered Christmas when he was a kid. The toughest part was waiting to get out of school. Squirming on the hard seats, trying to listen to the teacher and getting permission to leave the room every time he could get away with it.

He remembered sitting on the toilet and talking to the other kids up the line.

"What did you get your father?" he would ask.

"A dollar safety razor. Maybe now he will stop using his straight razor and throw away that strop."

"If he don't use the strop he'll use something else."

"Vincent's right. I lost my father's strop for him and now he beats me with an old shoe. I don't know which is worse."

"Hey, Vince, I'm getting a box of chocolate-covered cherries for my mother."

"My mother doesn't like candy."

"Mine doesn't either. But I do."

"That's a lousy trick."

"So what? My sister buys stockings for my mother. Then she takes them back during the year."

"Jiggers. Squeeze hard. Here comes O'Sullivan."

The principal walked slowly down the open booths and all the boys sat quietly with serious, straining faces.

"Weren't you here the last period?"

"Yes, Mr. O'Sullivan," he answered. "But I got a little cramp today."

The principal nodded and walked on. When they heard the door shut they started talking again.

"I wish we had a lady principal."

"More privacy."

"There goes the bell."

"Let's get back before class changes. So the next teacher will let us leave the room again."

There was the rustle of toilet paper. The sounds of toilets flushing and the groans as boys stood up on stiff cramped legs. "I'll be glad when school is over."

"Me too. This day before Christmas is hard on my ass."

When the final bell rang they screamed and raced across the school yard. They broke up into gangs. Bumped into girls. Knocked off hats. Jumped the fire hydrant. Then stopped off at the five and ten for a last look. Maybe buy a last present for some cousin, or steal a card off the rack for the girl downstairs.

Then he raced home to get out of his school clothes. And before going down to the cellar to find the Christmas tree decorations his mother gave him a glass of milk and a sandwich in the kitchen.

Their kitchen was like all the kitchens in Little Italy. With the shopping finally over, the cases of soda and the bottles of wine and the pots of soup filled the fire-escape. The broom closet was full of escarole, endives, romaine, tomatoes and big hot-house cukes.

All over the house there were bowls of fruit and nuts. When the bowls were empty there was plenty more in the linen closet. Oranges, tangerines, grapes. And soft McIntosh apples for the old people with no teeth.

Jammed on every shelf were cakes and cookies and pies. The kind of pastry Uncle Ralph liked. And the sponge cake for Grandma Fantino from Jersey. Sweet ones for the kids and the cheese cake you got to have because you never know who's going to drop in for coffee.

The oven was working away on the turkey and the roast. There were pots full of sauces singing and steaming. The icebox was jammed. And his mother walked around, her hair pulled back in a bun, in the clean house dress, with soft bedroom slippers on the feet thick with blue veins.

She was tired, but she was happy working alongside of the dreams of all her other Christmases.

When his sandwich was finished he got the decorations out and started on the tree. Each year he promised himself it would be the best, and when it was done he got his mother from the kitchen.

"But the lights, Vincent, they are all in the back."

"That's so the people in the street can see."

"And who is the tree for, Vincent? The family or the people outside?"

When he was washed and dressed he sat in the window and looked down the street waiting for his father to come home.

He could hear the door bells ringing in other flats and people coming up the stairs. It was the children who had moved away coming home for Christmas—the son who owned a tailor shop and lived in the Bronx, or the daughter from Rockaway whose husband sold insurance. They came up laughing and complaining about the stairs. Their hands were full of presents, bottles, cakes and more food. The grandchildren ran on ahead and threw themselves at Grandma.

He could hear the happy voices fill the hall.

"Boy, no house in the world smells so good, Ma. You make the ravioli the way I like?"

"Ma, you work too hard. You look tired."

"How you like the size of the kid? Next year he goes to school."

"Hey, who trimmed the tree? I ain't here and the tree looks like it got shoved out the window."

Then he saw the big cars come. The big cars from Westchester and Long Island. Some even had chauffeurs. They belonged to the kids who really went up. Coming home for Christmas—lawyers, designers, actors, singers.

Sometimes a mother from another flat would call his mother out in the hall.

"Mrs. Milazzo," the mother would say, her eyes wet with pride. "This is my boy Arthur. You remember him?"

"Sure I remember him."

"He's a doctor now."

"That's nice. He always was a good boy."

They said Merry Christmas all around and then his mother came back into the flat.

"Why do they show off like that?" he asked.

"Show off?" His mother smiled sadly. "From the first

time she shows her baby to the father until the day she dies a mother never gets tired of showing. I wait for the Christmas I can go into the hall and say my Vincent is a lawyer."

Then his father, loaded with packages, would come up the stairs and Christmas would really begin. They had supper. Then they sat around and talked. Tomorrow there would be cousins and aunts and uncles. But tonight it was just he and his father and mother and they told him stories of confirmations, graduations, weddings, and all the things that happen to a family.

"Look, Ma's crying."

"Every Christmas Ma cries."

"It's nothing. I'm happy I cry."

But the tears finally stop.

And that was the way Christmas came to Little Italy.

He sighed sadly. For him there would be no Christmas. His mother and father were dead and he wasn't a human being. He was a bull. A dick. A cop. And this was just another day. But not just another case.

Instead of peace on earth his heart was full of hate. He wanted to get Rocky Tosco.

He crossed the street and went into old man Bianco's candy store. The gray and white marble counter and the twist-around stools were the same as he remembered years ago. One whole side of the narrow store had soft-covered books and magazines. Behind the counter were shelves filled with headache powders, razor blades, pen wipers and key chains.

The old man's big mustache and puffy eyebrows had turned white, but that was all. He still held a little piece of cigar between his teeth. He still wore a stiff white jacket and had a painful flatfooted walk.

"Mr. Bianco."

"At's me."

"My name is Vincent Milazzo."

The old man looked him over carefully, then nodded. "I knew your father. A good man."

"Thanks."

"How's your mother?"

"She's been dead for ten years."

"Sure." The old man tapped his forehead. "I should of remembered."

"I'm with the police department now, Mr. Bianco."

He wasn't telling the old man anything new. The old man had placed him the moment he mentioned his name. Milazzo's kid. The one who became a cop.

"Mr. Bianco, what time did you get here this morning?"

"I told the other policeman. I get here maybe six-thirty. I drag in the case of milk and untie the papers and put them on the stand. Then I stay around with nothing to do. It's a lousy penny business. A piece of candy. A shoe lace. The kids steal more than I sell."

"There was a man murdered across the street this morning."

"Excuse me. I got a customer."

The old man went to the front of the store and started to make a malted for a taxi driver.

The old man knew all about the murder. A few seconds after the sound of the shot disappeared the word began to go around the street; up the stairs, down the halls, into the flats. Voices went low. Cups of coffee stopped halfway to the mouth. Razor blades stopped scraping. The women shook their heads sadly, and the men nodded wisely.

By now everyone knew. Everyone had figured why Tony was killed, and maybe even who did it. And they weren't often wrong.

Modern crime detection—that's what everybody harped

on: fingerprints, mud and blood stains, a piece of hair. Then clever deduction. It was for the comic books and the movies. He and the other detectives often laughed. It was their favorite joke. What good was all the science in the world if you didn't have a suspect to work it on. And the best way to get a suspect was with an eyewitness.

But better than all the records in Central, better than all the files in Washington with the tricky electric machines that sorted out the information, give him just one neighborhood gossip. A snoopy janitor who had insomnia, or a busybody who slept with her ear against the door. In a few minutes he could get more information from them than Central could dig up in a year.

He remembered how he broke that has-been actress killing last year. The usual naked body, the blue face, the marks on the neck and the little address book with over two hundred names. To check all those men and their alibis would have taken him and half the department six months. But with luck he broke the case in nine hours.

He smiled whenever he thought about it. He had gone up on the roof of the apartment house to get away from the howling reporters. He wanted to stand there in the fresh night air and think.

Then he saw it. A shadow on the roof across the way. He remembered the old line about a murderer returning to the scene of his crime.

He raced down the back stairs to duck the reporters, sneaked to the building across the street, and took the elevator up. He pulled out his gun and went on the roof.

Sitting there on a beat-up army blanket with a big pair of black binoculars was a pimply-faced, twelve-year-old kid.

When the boy was finally convinced he wasn't going to jail, he talked. No woman in that neighborhood could leave her shade up and squeeze out of her girdle, no girl could brush her teeth, without that kid knowing about it.

The ex-actress had been one of his favorite shows. She went on every night. And like a true trouper she liked lots of lights and the curtain up. From the kid's description he was able to finger the three current boy friends. Then science went to work and told him which suspect it was. After that, getting a confession was a snap.

He had promised the kid never to tell on him. And he didn't. When the reporters asked him how he cracked the case he told them the lab analyzed the stains on a sheet. The next morning all the papers raved about the brilliant, scientific laboratory work. And he'd just laughed.

Now if he could get old man Bianco or some of the other people in the neighborhood to open up and talk he could find out all about Tony and Rocky and the dirty pictures in a few minutes.

The cab driver finished his malted, paid and left. The old man walked back slowly.

"That's right, Mr. Bianco," he started again. "Tony Statella was murdered this morning."

The old man clicked his tongue sadly.

"Did you know Tony, Mr. Bianco?"

"Sure. He used to live on this street."

"Did you like Tony?"

"Another boy."

That meant he didn't like Tony. But it also meant Mr. Bianco had decided not to talk. Well, he knew the people of Little Italy. When they made up their minds not to talk it was best to save time and move on. It was a trick they carried over from Sicily. It was in their veins, but it was stronger than blood. Blood could spill, but a good Sicilian would never spill.

He tried something else.

"Mr. Bianco, you sell pictures?"

"What kind of pictures?"

"Pictures of girls getting undressed."

The old man spit on the floor.

"You got wrong store."

"Then you know what pictures I mean."

"I seen them."

"Where?"

The old man looked him over carefully. He was trying to decide how much it was right to tell a cop.

"A couple months ago," the old man finally said, "a man comes. He's got a box of dirty pictures. Costs me one dollar. I'm supposed to sell for one dollar fifty. But I don't sell dirty pictures."

"Was the man Tony Statella?"

"I don't know who was the man."

"I see. Mr. Bianco, do you know Rocky Tosco?"

"I know Rocky Tosco." The old man spit again.

So the old man hated Rocky too. That was good to know. If he rubbed the sore spot he might be able to shake something loose.

"That Rocky is a nice boy."

"Who?" The old man was surprised. "Rocky? Nice?"

"I thought you liked him. He and his gang always hung around here when they were kids."

"Yeah. He took money from his old man's cash register to buy things. Big-shot. That's the way he kept his friends—stealing from his old man."

"That was only kid stuff."

"Yeah," Mr. Bianco pulled the wet cigar from his mouth. "How about the time Rocky took that nine-year-old Capra girl to the cellar and got her drunk on wine?"

"Rocky was only fourteen himself."

"So what?" The old man threw the cigar on the floor. "It was a good thing they found them in time. Old man Capra gave it to Rocky good. Bang across the mouth. Bang on the head. Then old man Tosco comes running out of the butcher shop and sticks a knife in Capra's shoulder."

"Say, Mr. Bianco, was Rocky the guy who tried to sell you those dirty pictures?"

The old man's white eyebrows went up.

"What's a matter with me? You hate Rocky, and his father too. Sure, I remember. You and Rocky always fighting. You're trying to steam me up so I'll say things."

Well, that was it. He was finished here.

"No, Mr. Bianco. I came in for some pipe tobacco."

"Sure, what kind?"

"That ten-cent stuff over there."

He handed the old man a quarter. Then counted his change.

"Mr. Bianco. I gave you a quarter."

He held out his hand so the old man could see his change. "You owe me a nickel more."

"At's right. I'm getting old. Can't see so good."

He smiled as he left the candy store. The old man, like the street, hadn't changed much. Mr. Bianco wasn't a crook at heart. Short-changing people was his hobby. Excitement. Something to tell his friends about.

Once the old man short-changed a priest, and then it bothered him so much he chased two blocks to give it back. But to cheat a cop—that would be a real story. Well, if Bianco had talked more he would have let him keep the nickel. But he hadn't learned a thing.

He tried Gus at the grocery store. He tried the boys in the vegetable store. And he had a cup of coffee at the all-night restaurant, but even Pete, the gabby chef, wasn't talking.

They were fast enough to tell him they didn't like Tony Statella. They all had good reasons to hate Rocky Tosco. But when he mentioned dirty pictures or asked who Rocky knew to keep his place open they changed the talk to something else.

Well, there was another way for a cop to get information. A way so dirty cops didn't even talk about it much. But it was the way three-quarters of all cases were solved. It was as important to police work as bullets to a gun.

Stool pigeons—a cop's best friend.

There were all kinds of stoolies. Some of them wanted money or a favor, some wanted to get revenge. Most did it to keep the cops off their necks. In the name of justice a cop had to blackmail ex-cons, beat up bums, push prostitutes around—and give money to junkies so they could buy another veinful of death.

It was dirty and rotten, but that's the way it was. As much as he hated it, if he wanted to find out about Tony Statella and Rocky Tosco he'd have to go out and roast some pigeon.

The easiest kind of stoolie to work with was the squealer. The minute they heard of a robbery or killing they followed the cop on the case like a sparrow follows a horse on the bridle path. They slunk in doorways, waited in hallways, sneaked into the police station—wanting to give all kinds of important information, for a price. Most of the time it was worthless, but you had to listen, because sometimes they gave you what you were looking for.

With that kind it was just a matter of waiting until they found you. He looked at the big round clock in front of the jewelry store. It said nine-thirty. He'd give them twenty minutes.

He stood there watching the wind belly the big Christmas sign that hung over the street. A Salvation Army girl was setting up a box for collections on the corner. Further down the block a man was carrying a Christmas tree into a tenement house. He knew that dilapidated old house. How often he passed by looking up to the window on the second floor. That's where Gina Rossi lived and where a big piece of his heart was buried.

He was all lost in bitter memories when he heard the *pssst*. Like someone dropping cold water on hot steel. He turned slowly and looked. It was Minetta—money-mad Minetta.

He followed him.

Money-mad was a big, good-looking boy with black wavy hair and a neat little mustache. He could have been a dancing teacher or a rumba band leader. But he had a bone twisted somewhere in his head.

He was thrown out of the Army because he couldn't stop selling slightly used jeeps to the Arabs. In civilian life he sold slugs to use in subway turnstiles. He also went around with a cardboard container and collected dimes for the Englewood Orphanage of which he was president and sole orphan. In between Money-mad sold information.

The whole neighborhood knew about Money-mad, so his stuff wasn't so private. The only reason the punks let him live was because they figured if anyone was dumb enough to let Money-mad get anything on them they deserved to be arrested. Sometimes they even fed him crazy stories to confuse the cops.

As far as being used as a witness, no district attorney would touch him. He would promise to tell the truth, and then switch his story for two bucks. But Money-mad had big ears and you could never tell what transom he happened to be hanging over. So he had to listen to the guy.

Money-mad stopped in front of a tenement house, looked around, then went in. When he got to the house he banged the ashes out of his pipe and went in too.

There was another *pssst* from the darkness behind the stairs. He just leaned against the wall and waited. He didn't like to get too near Money-mad. Stoolies were hard on his stomach.

"I got real hot news, Detective."

"Yeah."

"Extra special news."

"Talk."

"Best news you ever heard."

"Okay." He knew what Money-mad was getting at. He dug into his pocket and came out with his wallet. He pulled out the few bills he had, rolled them over so they looked like more and waved them back and forth. Though he couldn't see his face in the dark he could almost hear Money-mad drool.

"Talk."

"Sure. Detective, I know who killed Tony Statella. It was a bricklayer."

"A bricklayer." He could feel his body go stiff. "What's his name?"

"That I don't know."

He relaxed.

"Your news stinks."

"Wait a minute. The bricklayer is a young guy. He lives right in the neighborhood. He had a fight with Tony over a dame. So he killed Tony."

The story didn't make much sense. Probably something Money-mad dreamed up for a buck.

"What do you know about Rocky Tosco?"

"Rocky? I got something extra special hot on him. I heard it a couple of months ago. Some guys were talking in a parked car near Rocky's restaurant. I happened to be sitting on the bumper and I heard. One guy was called Gale."

Gale. The name sounded familiar.

"Well," Money-mad said. "This Gale was talking how he and Rocky were in business together. An employment agency for girls. They sent them out on jobs all over the country."

"What kind of jobs?"

"Chorus girls. Strippers. Singers. Bar girls. Sounded like big-time stuff."

Then it clicked. It was probably Jim Gale. A dirty, bloated guy with a big hairy nose from the Chicago crowd. A phony press agent from the burlesque and honkytonk circuit. He had married a great big six-foot-three stripper and after shows he rented her out to his friends. Sweet Jim Gale. He and Rocky made a good pair.

"What else do you know?"

"That's all. Someone got into the car and they took off. How about my money?"

"One more thing. Who's Rocky's protection? Who does he pay off to keep his restaurant open?"

"That I don't know. I gave you all my news."

"What do you know about dirty pictures?"

He heard Money-mad gasp in surprise.

"Who ratted on me? I'll kill him!"

"Come on, spill."

"It ain't against the law. I buy them for a buck and sell them for a buck-fifty."

So even Money-mad was pushing the stuff.

"Where do you buy them?"

"From Handy Moore."

That was one of Tony Statella's regular boys. An un-graded moron who'd hock his mother's false teeth.

"What else do you know?"

"Nothing now. But I'll find you tomorrow and give you more."

"Your news stinks."

He pulled five dollars off his roll. Money-mad's hand darted out of the dark and snatched it away.

"Five bucks," Money-mad whined. "Five lousy bucks for all that hot stuff. Detective Scotti always gives me ten."

He grabbed into the darkness, caught hold of a piece of coat and yanked Money-mad out.

"Listen, punk," he said. "You tell Scotti I talked to you and I'll put you away for so long you'll spend your old-age benefits in jail."

"Why should I tell him, Detective? I ain't no squealer." He shoved Money-mad away so hard he slammed into the wall and plaster fell.

"Don't tell Scotti."

"Honest."

He started out, then stopped with a sigh. He opened his wallet and threw a five dollar bill on the floor.

Outside he took a deep breath of fresh air. He felt as if he just pulled his head out of a garbage can.

Ten bucks. That was the money for a pair of shoes next week. Maybe someday the Department would give them an expense account for paying stoolies. Or maybe he should ask for a receipt so he could take it off his taxes. What a filthy life.

He waited around for another few minutes, but no one tried to contact him. They were probably afraid of the neighborhood. Afraid to be seen talking to a cop. If it was dark they'd be crawling all over him, but he couldn't wait for night.

He started walking up the street. When he reached the corner he saw a cab, and sitting in the driver's seat was a guy with a familiar face. He jerked the cab door open and slipped into the back seat.

The cabbie put his magazine away.

"Where to, mister?"

"Keep your hand off the flag, Benny. We aren't going any place."

"Cheez, a cop!"

"What's new, Benny?"

"I ain't talking."

Benny was a weak-minded crowd follower. If the boys went out to rob an armored truck with a can opener Benny would tag along. If the fellows decided to push people off the Brooklyn Bridge, Benny would be lookout.

When Benny was a kid the gang he followed rolled a junkie in a hallway and found his kit. They sat around in a cellar looking at the stuff, wondering what it was really like. Then someone decided it would be fun to see how it worked. They called for volunteers and Benny laid out his arm.

The first time he just got sick. But three days later they tried again and it took. Benny was sillier than ever. The gang had their laughs and then they forgot about it. But not Benny. He couldn't forget that feeling of being bigger than God, that feeling of stepping out over the buildings and looking down on the crowds. It was great stuff, worth all the hot shakes and cold sweats that went with it.

Benny went on the needle. He sold his schoolbooks, used his lunch and movie money. He stole from his mother's pocketbook. He started hocking things out of the house.

When his family found out about it they raised the dough and sent Benny on a cure. Three weeks after he got home Benny climbed out on the needle and went flying over the city again. Every couple of years they put Benny on the cure. It kept his family broke. And it kept Benny a skinny skeleton. He lost weight, but he never lost the urge.

"You still on the needle, Benny?"

"Not for a year. I took the cure."

"Junkies aren't supposed to push cabs."

"I tell you I'm off the stuff."

"Let's see your arm, Benny. Let's see the tattoo mark your friend the needle left."

"Cheez, copper, go away, leave me alone. You cops are

always pushing me around. I don't bother no one."

What was he supposed to say? You're right, Benny. You're just a poor sucker and I feel sorry for you. No. He was a cop, and a cop wasn't supposed to have any feelings. A cop was just supposed to get the facts—and Benny was just supposed to be a source of information.

"Cheez, copper, getting in my cab in daylight, right in the neighborhood. You trying to get me marked stoolie?" Benny's eyes got wet. "They'll kill me."

"Turn around, Benny." He couldn't stand looking at the shrunken face with the scared eyes. "The faster you talk the faster I go."

Benny turned his face away and shrugged his bony shoulders. "Who killed Tony, Benny?"

"I was in the Uptown Garage this morning. I just heard about it myself. But I'll talk around. Let me pick you up in Brooklyn someplace tomorrow. Away from here. And I'll tell you what I found."

"No time, Benny. What do you know about Rocky Tosco?"

"If I tell you something will you get out quick and leave me alone?"

"It's a deal."

"A month ago I got a fare near the park. The girl was a young beaut. The guy was old—gray hair, real class. But I knew him from someplace. The old guy was talking about the girl needing singing lessons before she'd be ready for Broadway. The girl said something about not having enough dough. The old guy tells her since she's a friend of Rocky Tosco she doesn't have to worry. Well, that did it. The minute he said Rocky's name I remember the old guy. It was Alvin Allen."

"The con man?"

"That's right. They got off at Forty-ninth. And that's all."

Alvin Allen. A fancy-talking fake. The last time he heard Allen was in trouble milking a bunch of GIs out of their tuition with a phony dancing school. Rocky was certainly keeping funny company.

"What about dirty pictures, Benny?"

"I told you all I know."

"Benny, who does Rocky get his protection from? Who fixes it so he can sell liquor after hours?"

Benny turned his skinny face around. The tears were running down the deep creases to his bony chin.

"Stop wringing me, copper. Please get out before someone sees and marks me rat. I want to live."

"Okay. Okay."

Seeing a guy break down and cry made him feel sick. He got out of Benny's cab and started walking.

Then he suddenly pulled the pipe out of his mouth and shook his head. It had been so long since he worked the old neighborhood he had forgotten a good bet.

Rosa the Bag. She'd know plenty. He went back to the cab.

"Benny."

"Cheez. Not again."

"Ah, stop bawling. All I want to know is where can I find Rosa the Bag?"

"She's out of circulation. She don't work no more."

"Where does she live?"

Benny gave him an address a couple of blocks away. While he walked he remembered Rosa. She had been a pretty little kid. They'd been in the same class in school. Then Rosa started filling out her sweater. The bigger she got the more school she missed.

Pretty soon the whole neighborhood knew. At night little Rosa was climbing into Sam Weaver's moving truck. There among the old blankets they used to wrap around the furniture, Rosa was collecting quarters and then dollars.

She got herself silk stockings, a snazzy squirrel coat and sexy dresses. The kids called her Rosa the Bag but she was happy.

Then one day a couple of fellows talked her into one of the cellar clubs. There were around twenty guys waiting down there. They ruined her dress, dumped a bottle of beer in her hat and tore her squirrel coat. But what was worse, when it was over they shoved her out without a cent.

That's when Tony talked to her. He was older and he used a knife in a couple of fights so he had a reputation for being tough. With him around none of the guys would try to take her over again. And all it would cost was half her money. So Rosa became Tony's girl.

That was over fifteen years ago. Tony had been through plenty of other women since then, and Rosa had had other boy friends. But if he knew women, Rosa would still have a soft spot for her first man.

Rosa's apartment was on the top floor. When he knocked on the door she asked who it was.

"It's me," he said.

The door opened for a peek and he stuck his toe in.

"Let me in, Rosa."

"A cop!" She tried to close the door.

"Come on, Rosa," he said softly. "The landlord will be sore as hell if I smash his door."

"What do you want?"

"Let me in, Rosa."

She let go of the door and he went in.

Even in a housedress and flat shoes Rosa looked sexy. He looked around the clean little flat, then walked to an old fashioned rocking chair and sat down.

"You got no right here, copper." She stood in the middle of the room with her hands on her hips. "I'm a respectable married woman." When he didn't answer she got more courage. "My husband will go down to the station house and file a complaint. What's your badge number?"

He sighed as he pulled his badge from his pocket and held it out for her to see.

"Forget it." Her hands slipped from her hips. "I don't want to make you no trouble." Her courage was going. "Just beat it and I'll forget the whole thing."

He put the badge back and pulled out his pipe. He looked around for a place to dump the ashes. Rosa picked an ashtray off the table and handed it to him. It was a sea-shell souvenir from Coney Island. The date on it said it was ten years old.

"Tony Statella give it to you?"

"Please, Detective. My next-door neighbor is a trouble-maker. If you don't go right away she'll tell my husband that a man was in the apartment."

He finished filling his pipe and he lit it.

"If you want money," her voice went hard, "I haven't any. He gives me two dollars a day to feed him and his three kids. That's all I get."

He sat there smoking his pipe as if she wasn't in the room.

"Well, keep your eyes off the bedroom doors." She was shouting now. "I cut all that stuff out."

He blew smoke at the ceiling.

"Oh, God, what the hell do you guys want from me?" Rosa sat down on a chair and started to cry. Then slowly she looked up.

"I got eighteen dollars in an oatmeal box. Take it."

He didn't answer and after a while she tried again.

"If I let you come in the bedroom will you go away quick and never come back again?"

"You got me wrong, Rosa."

"Then what?"

"Information."

"Why don't you cops stop hounding me? Always riding me. If it's not one thing, it's another. Last week it was that Detective Scotti. Always squeezing me. I'm no stool pigeon."

"I want to know about Tony."

"He's dead. What's to know?"

"Who killed him?"

"Some young kid. A bricklayer who was working for the government in Alaska. When he came back he found his girl mixed up with Tony. So he killed him."

There it was again. The same story. If it was true his case against Rocky Tosco was dead. But he couldn't give up that easy. Maybe it was a plant. Maybe Rocky himself was sending the story around the street. He was sneaky enough to pull a trick like that.

"Who told you, Rosa?"

"Everybody is talking." Rosa shrugged. "The janitor, the snoopy dame next door. Now will you blow? If she tells my man you were here he'll kill me."

"Were you and Tony still friends?"

"Are you kidding? I bought him his first two-dollar tie. Now he wears Fifth Avenue originals. He's real class."

"Was. He's dead now."

"Yeah." She sighed sadly. "Poor Tony."

Women. He wanted to spit. Tony used to wait in the hall until she was finished. Then he'd take his share of the money and buy other girls drinks. When Rosa got old he pushed her away for someone younger. Yet she still sighed for the guy.

Why did women fall for potatoes like that? Even a smart kid like Gina Rossi made a fool out of herself with Rocky. Women. There was no use trying to figure them out.

"What was Tony's latest business?"

"Tops," Rosa said. "Tony bought in on a black book."

"Whose black book?"

"Don't ask me, but they were peddling it for a hundred thousand dollars."

"A hundred thousand?"

"Sure. That book was worth it—over four hundred names, the richest men in the world. Guys who were willing to give five hundred dollars for a night with the right girl."

"That's a lot of money."

"I go nuts when I think how I used to do it for quarters."

"The price of everything has gone up these days."

"Yeah." Rosa laughed.

"Where did Tony get all that money?"

"It wasn't only him. It was a syndicate. They put in money for shares."

"Who were the others?"

"I heard Brown was one."

"Which Brown?"

"Sammy Brown, of Hollywood."

"But selling women isn't his line. He's a blackmailer."

"Well, he was one of them. Rocky Tosco was another. And that's all I know."

He took the pipe out of his mouth and leaned forward.

"What do you know about Rocky?"

"Did you ever see his muscles?" Rosa asked. "Strong as a bull, and he's rough with women."

"Yeah." He thought of Rocky and Gina Rossi and the hate started building up. "The hell with his sex life. What about his business?"

"The syndicate used Rocky's restaurant for showing the girls to some of the clients. A guy could drop down there and pick who he wanted."

"Is Rocky the top man of the syndicate?"

"I don't know who's the head, but Rocky is only small change."

"And the dirty pictures?"

"I don't know anything about that."

"One more question. Who is Rocky's connection? How is he getting protection to run his joint wide open?"

"I don't know that either. You got to get out now. My husband is very jealous. Last week he gave me hell on account of Detective Scotti."

"What does Scotti take? Money or the bed?"

"He's like you. He wants information. All cops want something. Just because I made a few mistakes I got to pay all my life. Why don't you guys let up? Honest, I'm human, just like you."

"Who told you cops were human?" He got up and went to the door. "Squeezing junkies and pushing prostitutes is our business, because good citizens won't talk."

"Good citizens," Rosa sneered. "Listen, cop. There are only two kinds of people in this world. Crooks, and those that don't get caught."

"Yeah." He opened the door. "I'm sorry I had to break in."

"Forget it," Rosa said. Then she poked a finger at him. "But don't come back."

In the hall he heard the door across the way click shut. Rosa wasn't kidding. Her neighbor was on the prowl. Chances were Rosa would get an argument that night.

He walked down the stairs and out into the street thinking about it. He had parlayed a set of dirty pictures into a crime syndicate that reached from Little Italy to Broadway to Fort Wayne to Hollywood.

Besides a restaurant it had a photography studio, an employment agency, a singing school and a black book worth a hundred thousand dollars.

There was a press agent who sold his own wife, a con man, a blackmailer, and Rocky. He felt as if he was stumbling around in a cesspool. Given a couple of days he

could break the thing wide open. But he was Detective
Milazzo of Homicide. Murder was his business. Who'd
killed Tony Statella? And that was all.

Even when he found the murderer and arrested him, it
didn't mean a thing. There were lots of holes between
booking a guy and watching him take a sentence.

One day he caught a punk standing over a body with
the gun still smoking in his hand. There were six reliable
witnesses. A case couldn't be tighter. But by the time it
got to court the witnesses forgot what they saw. The
lawyer from the District Attorney's office asked the wrong
questions. And the ballistics experts said the gun didn't
do the killing. The guy got off.

It could have been political pressure from the mayor's
office. It could have been a deal swung through the D.A.
It could have been worked through the judge. And sometimes evidence and papers were lost right in the police department.

The arresting cop never knew exactly how and who
broke his case. All he knew was to keep his mouth shut
and go back to his work.

But if a cop stepped out of line—if he moved into another department's territory like Division or Safe and
Loft—then he was asking for trouble.

He would be called in and told to lay off. He wasn't
supposed to be a one-man vice campaign. If he kept on
anyway he would find a notice on the bulletin board bust-
ing him down to a patrolman. And if he still gave trouble
and the opposition was tough enough the cop could turn
a corner one day and find a bullet waiting for him. And
everybody would say he asked for it. He should have
minded his own business.

Murder. He sighed. Two weeks ago he had to book an
old man who'd given his wife a dose of poison. She was
sixty-eight and slowly rotting away with cancer. The old

man couldn't stand to see her suffer any more. That was murder.

Then there was the hysterical woman of forty, sitting at the edge of the bed in her nightgown looking at her husband. She had stuck a scissors in his back while he slept because he was going to divorce her for a younger girl. She was so dazed they almost had to carry her down to book her. She was a murderess.

But Rocky and Jim Gale and the others—they weren't murderers. They had good lawyers, and good connections.

Well, he was tired of it all. He was going to get the hell out of the whole mess. Get some fresh air in his lungs, some sun in his face. Maybe he'd take a job pushing a long distance truck on the highway, or even take his Uncle Joe's offer to skin fish on the wharf.

But before he quit there was one thing he had to do. Get Rocky Tosco. Send him to the chair. Watch him squirm and fry. Otherwise he would never be able to get a good night's sleep.

He had to get Rocky Tosco—even if he had to frame him.

When he got to the corner he saw the police car with Whiteman sitting in it. He got into the car and started to light his pipe. Then he put it away. His mouth was bitter. It could be from too much smoking, or maybe the life he was leading.

"I left the girl at Central," Whiteman said. "She's looking at the pictures."

"I have a hunch she doesn't find the right man."

"She seemed sure of herself. I also cased the store that sells the strip pictures. It's a hole in the wall, but it's right on the Avenue, next to a penny arcade and a girlie show. They have the pictures in cellophane and stuck in racks.

Dollar-fifty a set. I clocked the place for a half hour. Twenty-one guys came out. I couldn't tell how many sets they bought."

"Would you say they bought a set apiece?"

"Oh, sure. Some came out with packages of the stuff."

"Any idea how long the store stays open?"

"The sign said from ten to ten, seven days a week."

"And that's a lively neighborhood."

"It's moving day and night."

"Well, Whiteman, did you figure how many pictures they sell?"

"I was never good at arithmetic."

"Hang onto your underwear. Twelve hours a day, three hundred and sixty-five days a year. At one set to a customer, it brings the total to over a quarter of a million dollars a year."

"From a couple of dirty pictures? You're kidding."

"That's the figure. And that's only one hole in the wall. There's probably at least one place like that in every city. But let's say there's only a thousand in the whole country. That means over two hundred and fifty million dollars a year."

"I'm getting sick," Whiteman said.

"Just some dirty pictures. That's what people say. But organized right, it becomes big industry."

"We're in the wrong racket," Whiteman said sadly. "Oh, here's something you'd like to see. They found it in Tony's apartment."

Whiteman gave him some brown envelopes held together with a rubber band. He opened one of the envelopes and there were negatives in it. Negatives of a girl getting out of her clothes. He looked through the other envelopes. All girls getting undressed. The fourth envelope stopped him.

"Hey, Whiteman. Look at these."

Whiteman held them up and looked.

"Nice legs."

"The face. Recognize her?"

"Yeah. Sure," Whiteman said. "That's the blonde kid I just took down to Central."

Tony told the kid he had destroyed the negatives for her. And what about the other negatives. He took them out and looked more carefully. Then he placed another girl. He'd seen her singing on television. Another girl was starring in a Broadway play. He couldn't place any more, but it was a sure bet that they were all girls who'd made good.

"The rats," he told Whiteman. "A quarter of a billion dollars on dirty pictures isn't enough. They're banging away at blackmail too."

"Talking about rats," Whiteman said, "a cop's best friend paid me a visit."

"A pigeon?"

"Yeah. It cost me five bucks to get the news." Whiteman held out his hand.

"If it was Money-mad Minetta you're out your five bucks. He already told me the same thing for ten."

"That bastard. That's the second time he's pulled that trick on me." Whiteman laughed. "The next time I see him I'll take it out of his skin."

"Well, what do you think of his story?"

"To me it clicks. Whoever shot Tony in the ear was mad. A guy sore over his girl would do it. And it checks with what the blonde told me on the way down to the station."

"I think it's a lie. A plant to throw us off."

"Why?"

"Say it's a hunch."

Whiteman looked him over carefully.

"You mean, Vincent, you want to think it's a lie."

"Look, Whiteman, I just ran a couple of dirty pictures into a quarter of a billion dollar racket. Also a little bit of prostitution, blackmail and some larceny."

"You're supposed to find out who killed Tony Statella. Not start a one-man-clean-up-vice drive."

"What if I can tie all this stuff into the murder? What if can prove that one of the partners in the syndicate did the killing to go up a notch?"

"Would the partner be Rocky Tosco?"

"Yeah."

"And you mean you're going to frame him?"

"I didn't say that."

"No, Vincent. But I know what cooks in that head of yours. Being a cop isn't enough. Now you want to be a judge, jury and the guy who sends the juice through the hot seat. Take my advice. This job is too personal. It will get you in trouble. Hand it over to someone else."

"You know where you can put your advice."

"Look, Milazzo." Whiteman's heavy hand fell on his arm. "Last few months the whole department has been talking about how sour you're getting. Today you're so mean you're rotten. You been talking to people like they were dogs. The only reason I'm taking it is because I understand you."

He shook Whiteman's hand off his arm.

"What's to understand?"

"Every young cop goes through it, Vince. At the beginning everything is simple. There is a law. People who keep it are all right. People who break it are punished."

"I'm going to sleep, Whiteman."

"Then one day the cop finds out he's wrong," Whiteman went on, as if he hadn't heard. "The law isn't so simple. It's got holes in it so big a smart lawyer can walk elephants through them. People who keep the law don't have to be good, and sometimes a guy breaks the law and he deserves a medal. The picture gets all mixed up."

"Look, Whiteman. I'm not mixed up. I watched Rocky cheating on tests in school. I saw him stealing baby carriages out of cellars. I heard how he bought a rating and a desk job in the Navy. Then when he got out I saw him work his way up to big-shot. He gets whatever he wants. Cars. Clothes. And the nicest girls in the neighborhood. Well, I'm tired of it. I'm going to stop him. And now I'm going to get a cup of coffee."

"Vincent." Whiteman's hand was on his arm again. "Listen. To you Rocky isn't a person anymore—he's a system. Either his way is wrong and you're right, or his way is right and you've wasted your life. And once and for all you want to find out, even if you have to frame him. But if you frame him, you'll only be framing yourself."

"Stop preaching."

"Relax, Vincent. I'm going to tell you my story. I never told it before, not even to my wife—how I wanted to frame a guy, and when that didn't work I planned to kill him."

"It better be good." He took out his pipe and lit it.

"Years ago," Whiteman said. "When I was working on narcotics I got a tip from a stoolie. I broke into a flat and on the bed was a suitcase with half a million dollars' worth of uncut junk. The suitcase belonged to a monkey called Danny Sampson.

"'Look cop,' Sampson says to me. 'Forget you found the stuff and there's thirty thousand dollars cash in my wallet you can have.'

"Thirty thousand." Whiteman shook his head sadly. "Just the sound of that much money made me dizzy. I was making sixty a week after deductions. And all I had to do was reach in the guy's pocket to make thirty thousand.

"'Go ahead,' this Sampson keeps saying. 'Take out my wallet and count it.'

"But not me," Whiteman said. "I ain't rock. If I looked at the stuff, if I touched it—thirty thousand dollars! I'd never be able to put it back. I slammed the suitcase shut and dragged the guy down the street.

"Well," Whiteman said. "All the way to the station that monkey keeps telling me what I could buy with the money. All I had to do was close my hand and it was mine. Instead I slapped Danny Sampson across the chops to shut him up."

Whiteman stopped to look down at his big hands.

"Well," Whiteman said. "When I booked Sampson they went through his pockets and it was there like he said. Will you believe me, Vincent, when I tell you that I got sick watching them count out the dough. I had to go to the toilet and lay my head against the cold tile wall.

"But that would have passed," Whiteman said sadly. "The thing that hurt was Sampson got off. How? Who knows? A political connection; maybe someone in the mayor's office. Anyway, the case was thrown out. And the snow? Half a million dollars' worth of dream drug. Enough to flood every school in the country for a year, that sort of disappeared.

"What could I do?" Whiteman asked. "I was just a cop. I had to keep my mouth shut. Then one night I saw him. He was getting out of a big black convertible to go into a fancy nightclub. He had a flashy babe on each arm. My buddy Sampson—free as a bird to spread his poison and spend his money, and me a flatfoot working the soles off a six-dollar pair of shoes. Then Sampson saw me and laughed.

"'Hey,' Sampson said to the girls. 'That's an honest cop over there. Take a good look. Believe me, there aren't many.'"

Whiteman banged a fist into his hand. "That laugh followed me down the street. It followed me home. I heard it in my dreams. Honest cop. Honest cop. Thirty thousand dollars to make a pinch and the guy laughs in my face."

"Yeah, Whiteman. I guess I know how you felt."

"I used to walk down crowded streets and hear that bastard laughing in my ears. Drilling through my head. I started to drink, but it didn't help; instead it made me think of how to get the rat. Arrest him some night and plant an envelope of coke in his pocket? But he'd beat the rap again. Maybe I'd shoot him down and say he resisted arrest. But the big boys would know. They'd break me out of the force. So I just kept on drinking and thinking."

Whiteman laughed. It was an ugly laugh. "Drinking on my salary and buying groceries for the wife and two kids didn't work. I was in hock to my ears. They took the car away. They took the furniture away and the wife took the kids to her mother. And me? I tried to stay so drunk I couldn't hear a laugh. Then one night I picked up a bookie. On the way to the station house he shoved a hundred-dollar bill into my pocket."

Whiteman put his big hands on the steering wheel and squeezed so hard his knuckles turned blue.

"A hundred isn't thirty grand. And I won't give you any hearts and flowers. I opened up the door and let the bookie out. In my mind I was going to get my wife and kids out of hock. But going up the stairs with the dirty money I got ashamed. You ever been ashamed, Vincent?"

"I think I know what you mean."

"No, you don't. That's why I'm telling you this, Vincent. I don't want it to happen to you. I sold out my life for a hundred bucks. I was bringing the dirty money to my wife. That laugh in my ears grew so loud I almost went deaf. I turned around and got drunk. One hundred dollars' worth. It went that way for six months, until one day the bookie pointed me out in the line-up."

Whiteman took his hands off the steering wheel and studied them as if he had never seen them before.

"It was during the war. Cops were hard to get. They busted me down and gave me a thirty-day suspension. I was broke—no money, no wife. I was sitting around trying to get the courage to blow my brains out when I heard the news. Someone pushed Danny Sampson off the thirty-fourth floor of a building to splash all over the sidewalk."

Whiteman sighed and shoved his hands into his coat pockets.

"The steam went out of me. The pressure left my brain. There was still a God, and I'd been a stupid cop. I borrowed some money from my brother and got the family out of hock. Now when I look back it's all a bad dream. But the mark on my record is still there. And wise guys like you look down on me. That's all right. I made a mistake; I deserve it. But don't you do it. Stay away from Rocky. He's someone else's job."

They were quiet for a few minutes. Then finally he took the pipe out of his mouth.

"Look, Whiteman, maybe I've been wrong. But no matter what anyone says, I got to get Rocky."

Whiteman shrugged his shoulders. Then they sat there in the quiet. But the air was too stiff. He jerked the door open and got out.

"I'm taking a walk, Whiteman. I want to think."

He started down the street and he felt rotten. He knew Whiteman was right, but he couldn't help it. He had waited twenty years for God to act, and nothing had happened. Now he was going to do it himself. He was going to wipe that cocky grin off Rocky's face.

"Detective Milazzo?"

"Yeah." He turned around to look at a tall, dark fellow.

"My name's Scotti." The fellow held out his hand. "Detective Scotti of Division."

He looked at the hand for a second. Then he reached out and shook it.

"How about a cup of coffee, Milazzo?"

He followed the young detective into the coffee pot. He had to admit Scotti was a nice, clean-looking boy. Wavy hair, good face, the kind you found yourself wanting to like. They sat down at the counter and Scotti ordered two coffees.

"Heard a lot about you, Milazzo. The neighborhood is proud of you."

"Stop the soap."

"Okay." Scotti had a nice laugh too. "What I wanted to talk to you about was that killing this morning."

The counterman shoved two cups of coffee in front of them. He started to put some sugar in as he wondered what Scotti was up to.

"Well, I got something from a pigeon, Milazzo. I thought I'd pass it on. You know, one hand washes the other."

"My hands are clean. So if you're building up to a deal, take back your coffee."

Scotti laughed again.

"You're as tough as they say. But I have no deal. I just wanted to tell you who killed Tony Statella."

"I'm listening."

"A young kid who lives across the street. A stonemason. He was working in Alaska on a government project. When he got home he found Tony Statella was blackmailing his girl friend with some naked pictures. The kid went to get the pictures back. And when Tony said no, the kid killed him."

"Nice and simple. I bet you got the story from Rocky Tosco."

"Where I got it is my business, but I'm giving it to you."

"I don't believe the story. It's something Rocky Tosco is

planting around the street. There isn't any bricklayer."

"Why argue with me?" Scotti pushed his coffee away and stood up. "Why don't you check for yourself?"

"Every bricklayer in the city?"

"No. I'll give you his name."

His name! If Scotti knew the guy's name, it was legitimate. Then the blonde hat check girl, and the neighborhood, and Whiteman were right. Everybody was right. And he was wrong.

"What's the guy's name?"

"Pete," Scotti said. "Pete Rossi."

He watched Scotti pay the counterman and leave the restaurant. And all he could do was sit there and look at his coffee.

So now he knew who killed Tony—the young hardworking kid he knew so well. Pete Rossi. Gina Rossi's kid brother. He had to go out and arrest him and send him to the chair.

Then in the cup of coffee he saw Rocky's face. And Rocky was grinning.

PART TWO

He walked up the stairs to the second floor and knocked. The old lady opened the door.

"Hello, Mrs. Rossi."

"Hello, Officer Milazzo."

All the years he had been Vincent to her. Now he was Officer Milazzo.

"May I come in?"

She opened the door and he followed her to the kitchen.

"Sit down," she said. "Have a piece of cake and some coffee."

He didn't want any, but with the old lady it was habit.

Let her keep doing it. Let her have something to hang onto or she'd break down.

He sat there watching how she took the cup from the hook on the shelf and how her hand shook as she poured the stuff. What was he dragging it out for?

"Where's Pete, Mrs. Rossi?"

"Pete? He is not here, Detective."

If the old lady said so it was the truth. Pete was hiding out somewhere else and he was smart enough not to tell his mother where. The old lady wouldn't be able to lie. Not even to save her son.

"Where's Gina?"

"Gina? She is not here too."

"Will she be back?"

"Maybe in a minute. Maybe an hour."

That was it. If Gina wasn't working she had taken her kid brother someplace to hide. He would have to get it out of her. He took a swallow of coffee and got up.

"The cake is no good?"

"I'm sorry, Mrs. Rossi. I've got to go."

Out on the street it was getting colder. A raw wind was coming in from the river and the sky was angry gray. But he'd rather wait for Gina on the stoop and freeze than stay in the house and look at the old lady's face.

Gina Rossi. Even the name was like music. They were sixth or seventh cousins. Their mothers came from the same village in Sicily. In the old days the families got together every few months. And on Sundays little Gina came to visit his mother.

That was before the war. He was going to City College in the evening and doing part-time work on the docks during the day. One of the union officials had known his father and made sure he got enough jobs.

But lugging those crates and bags all day and then school and study at night took it out of him. So Sunday afternoons he left for relaxing. To just sit in front of the radio and take it easy.

Then Gina would come out of the kitchen to say hello. Little Gina who always seemed to have outgrown her dress, and whose long, skinny legs seemed to have outgrown her sweet little-girl face.

She asked questions about college, about the docks. She asked questions about everything. When he stopped answering she just went on talking, until he finally told her to keep quiet so he could listen to the radio. Then her face got sad and she stopped talking.

But she still didn't give him any peace. She stared. Those great big, dark brown eyes went all over him. Finally he put on his shoes and shirt and went out for a walk.

When he came home he asked his mother why that kid pestered him all the time. His mother smiled.

"She is in love."

"Love. Fourteen years old. She's a baby."

"True," his mother said. "But babies have hearts too."

Then one day on the docks they were swinging sugar out of the hold of a ship when a sling snapped. Someone hollered "heads up," and it started raining hundred-pound bags of sugar.

As he ducked he tripped over a rope. When he tried to get up he realized his ankle was sprained.

The compensation doctor told him to get the swelling down with cold compresses and come back in a few days to have it taped.

The moment Gina heard she came to the house.

"I'll put the compresses on, Vincent," she said.

"No you don't, Florence Nightingale. My mother will do it."

"How mean you are!" Her dark eyes flashed. "Your poor mother irons your shirts, washes your laundry, cleans the house and cooks. And you won't let me help."

"Okay! Okay!"

All that day he watched her move around the room. He watched her graceful hands wring the towels. He watched her slender fingers fold them around his ankle. Once when she leaned over to straighten the covers he watched her firm young breasts pull against her blouse.

He was shocked by his thoughts. Gina was only a baby—a cousin, a friend of the family.

But he couldn't get rid of the thought of Gina as a woman. And Gina walked around with a smile on her rich lips as if she knew exactly what was going on in his mind.

"You know, Vincent," she said. "My mother was sixteen years old when she got married."

"So?" he asked suspiciously.

"Do you think that's too young to marry?"

"It's too late to ask me now. Your mother's been married for twenty years."

"Oh, Vincent."

Then she brought him a tray of food and while she put it on his lap her body brushed his arm and he jerked away.

"What's wrong with you, Vincent?"

"Why don't you leave me alone?"

She looked hurt and then she smiled.

"All right, Vincent. I'm patient. I'll wait."

For a second he was going to ask her what she meant. But he didn't. He knew too well what she meant.

The next day he called a friend to get him down to the doctor's office.

"That's a bad sprain," the doctor said. "You should have stayed home another day. If you put weight on that foot too quickly you'll be in trouble."

"If I stay home another day I'll be in worse trouble."

Soon after that he went into the Army. Gina still visited

his mother. He knew that because of the letters—the words were his mother's, but the handwriting was Gina's. Sometimes she added a little P.S., like "I graduated this week."

One letter had a picture in it. A picture of his mother and Gina standing in front of a pigeon coop on the roof.

"Who's the girl alongside of your mother?" the fellows all asked.

"A kid from the neighborhood."

"Some kid. She's a beauty."

He trimmed the edges off the picture so it fit into his wallet. And sometimes, late at night, when he was in charge of quarters, he took out the picture and looked at it.

Then he got the sad letter. This time both the handwriting and the words were Gina's. His mother had died. He never answered the letter. Every now and then Gina sent him cigarettes or a card. He never got around to answering them either. What was there to say?

After the Army he didn't go back to the old neighborhood. There was nothing left but bitter memories. Instead he took a furnished room near Eighty-sixth Street and went back to college.

When he got his diploma he found it was only half the fight. To get a decent job you had to have connections or experience. He didn't have either.

Some of the other fellows in the same fix were talking about Civil Service—clean work, regular vacations, sick leave, pension. It spelled security, and it sounded good.

He checked all the lists and finally picked the Department. He took special courses at night, and five days a week he worked out in a gym.

The test was brutal. He chewed pencils until his teeth hurt, and he scratched his head until his scalp ached. But he passed. Then he took the physical and he was set.

Vincent Milazzo, Patrolman.

He drew the toughest assignment in the book. Harlem.
It wasn't only the uniform they resented up there—it was
also the color of his skin. He could see it in their eyes, feel
it in the way they talked. The resentment crawled out of
the sidewalks and hung over the streets.

He felt sorry for the people. But that didn't take the
chill off his back when he walked down those empty
streets at three in the morning. That crazy shake he got in
the legs every time he turned a corner and saw some street
lights were out. Was the bulb finished? Or had some
young punks knocked them out so it would be dark.
Young punks like animals, behind cars or in the halls,
waiting to come charging out.

An arm lock on the windpipe. A knee in the stomach. A
hundred hands cutting, slashing, pulling rings off fingers,
emptying pockets. Then off into the darkness, leaving
nothing but silence and a body.

His gun, his badge, his uniform—nothing could keep
the fear away. But he made himself walk down those dirty
streets. And on his days off he dreamed about getting a
transfer.

He had other dreams, too. Once while going through
his things he found the old picture of his mother and
Gina. He thought about calling her up. Maybe she was
married by now; if not he could take her out.

Then he counted his money. After deductions and rent
and food he had four dollars left. Where could he take
Gina on four bucks? No, he had to wait until he went up.
When he got to be a detective he'd be making more money
and he'd have more security. Until then he had no right to
think about girls.

The second year he got some breaks. They all came together in a streak. He picked up a guy who was wanted
for murder. A week later he chased and tackled a big
bruiser who had stuck an ice pick into a grocer's throat.

And then he got the drop on three armed punks who were looting a warehouse.

There were write-ups in the papers, some nice letters, and best of all, a promotion.

Vincent Milazzo. Detective Third Grade of Division.

But with the good came the bad. For his new assignment he was sent back to the old neighborhood. It took courage to face them.

The hellos were cold, the smiles stiff. At first he thought they hated him because he was a cop. Then he understood. They were waiting.

"The coffee is on the house, Detective," the guy in the coffee pot told him.

"No, thanks," he answered and shoved his money across the counter.

"A piece of fruit, Detective?" the vegetable man asked.

"No, thanks. I just finished eating."

They were testing. Finding out if he was going to be all right. Someone they could be proud of and respect, or a bum. A cheap potato who used the uniform to freeload.

"It's a detective."

"Are you sure?"

They said it loud so he would hear. A gang of tough teenage cowboys standing on a corner. If he went on like he hadn't heard they'd get louder and worse. If he went back and lost his temper the whole neighborhood would know about it.

He walked over and looked at them. They stood there staring back, waiting to see who would break first, who would make a fool of who.

"You guys are out of my class," he finally said. "I don't handle the baby-carriage trade."

"Baby carriage," a voice piped up. "Listen to him."

"Yeah, listen to me," he said slowly. "Or I'll sic the truant officer on you."

As he walked away they laughed. But not at him. They were laughing at themselves. They knew he had their number.

And that's the way it went day after day, test after test. Walking the tight line of the neighborhood's opinion. In a way it was as hard on his stomach as walking the lonely streets of Harlem.

But slowly the smiles got warmer. The hellos began to mean something. The word was getting around.

"Milazzo's son is all right."

"He'll make a good cop yet."

"Why shouldn't he? His father and my father played bocce together."

Vincent Milazzo. A straight cop.

He'd be a liar if he said it didn't make him feel good. He stood taller and walked straighter. Being a cop was getting in his blood. He was doing a job, and he was proud.

Sometimes he passed Gina on the street. She hadn't married yet, and she was twice as pretty as the picture, with those big brown eyes and that soft, rich skin. He'd look at her and forget to talk. And when he finally opened his mouth the words came out stiff. Then he'd say so long, and hurry off.

What else could he do? He found out that being a Detective Third Grade was just a fancy name for office boy. The few bucks more he got went for extras like carfare. And as far as security, third grade meant nothing. An order posted on the bulletin board and he'd be back on a beat.

But the next jump would be the real one. Detective Second Grade and he could really talk to Gina and have something to say.

But the next jump was the hard one. Being a real detective wasn't a matter of breaking a few cases or making a spectacular pinch. It took more and more work. There was a lot to learn—things you never found in a book.

You had to know your politics. Who you could trust in your own department, who controlled what, and where the leads were. You had to know the big boys and what strings they held. You had to know who belonged where and how far you could push.

But most important of all were the stoolies. A cop was no better than his source of information. Besides the junkies, the prostitutes, the psychopaths, the ex-cons, there were the undercover pigeons. That's where the real news was.

But the older cops were as jealous and protective of their private pigeons as a mother tiger with her cubs. Their stoolies were their bread and butter. A detective would rather have his tongue pulled out than give his stoolie away.

He soon learned a young cop had to go out and make his own contacts. He learned other things too, but he didn't learn fast enough.

One day in the barber shop he heard them talking about Gina Rossi. What a nice girl she was but now she was hanging out with Rocky Tosco. He couldn't believe it. But the guy talking seemed to know what he was saying. He got up.

"But, Detective," the barber said, "I'm not finished."

"Forget it, Tony."

He paid and hurried out into the street. He stood on the corner for three hours until he saw her coming home from work.

"Gina."

She turned around, saw him and gave him a big sunny smile.

"Hello, Vincent." It was like music.

For a moment his tongue was all knotted. Then he spit it out.

"You going around with Rocky Tosco?"

"I went out with him. Why?"

"He's no good. Stay away from him, or you'll be hurt."

"Rocky has been a perfect gentleman." Her smile was gone. Her big brown eyes had little fiery points of anger. "Even if he wasn't, what makes you think you have the right to talk to me like this?"

"Look, Gina. I'm telling you for your own good. Stay away from him."

"Is that all you have to say?"

"Yes. That's all I have to say."

She turned and walked away.

And that was the day he decided he was learning how to be a cop too slowly. What was he waiting for? He couldn't expect a girl like Gina to be around forever. He had to make his break. Get up there where he wanted to be. Then he could find Gina and tell her what was really on his mind.

That night he pinched Al Walsh, the gambler. Halfway to the station house he pulled up to the curb and parked.

"I hear you've been having tough luck, Al," he said.

"If it's money you want all I got is twenty bucks."

"I don't want your money. I want to give you some."

"What?" Al's wet blue eyes almost dropped out of his head.

"That's right, Al. You're good with the cards. You got a good reputation with the top boys. But like all gamblers you have ups and downs. Now you're down. I want to help you up."

"Ah, stop kidding me, Milazzo."

"On the level, Al. I want you to open up a card game in my territory. Any place you pick—back of a store, an empty flat. I'll give you cover. I'll see you're not pinched."

Al Walsh banged his forehead with his fist.

"I'm dreaming," he said.

"I want you to draw in the big boys. The inside crowd."

"And you?" Al Walsh was getting a shrewd look. "What kind of a cut do you get?"

"No money."

"That I can't believe."

"All I want is information."

"Me? A stoolie? You're crazy."

"Take your time, Al. Think it over."

He took Al to the station house and booked him.

Three days later he picked Al up again and asked if he had changed his mind. Al still wanted no part of it. So he booked him again.

He hounded Al. Six times in four weeks he ran him in, until Al was getting bowlegged. The poor guy finally broke down.

Al Walsh opened his game in back of a shoe store. One table, three good boys to deal and no limit. Every time the cop on the beat turned the place in he would make out a report saying he checked the address and no game was in progress.

What did he care about a couple of guys gambling? He was after bigger things—and he got them.

Al Walsh's place made itself a good name. The boys could relax while they played cards and not worry about getting caught in a cheap pinch. And as they took off their jackets and rolled up their sleeves to play cards they talked.

"What do you think of the Boston jewelry job?"

"That Sammy Hank is a good man to figure a layout."

"Yeah. But Green gets the credit for handling the steel box. It was a tough one. My cousin Solly Berg drove the car. He told me."

"Who's taking the stuff?"

"A fence in Philly. Otto Fantastic."

Or sometimes a couple of players pulled out of a deal to

take a container of coffee and a sandwich. While they ate they talked.

"I hear Nickie Real is back in town."

"Yeah. It means trouble for Looie Katz."

"The way I see it, Katz is fed up and Nickie better go home before he gets hurt."

"All that noise over a redhead."

"Yeah. She must have a new way to do it. Two hep gees like that gunning each other over a bag."

Gossip. That's all it was. Like a small town where everybody knows everybody else. That was the underworld. A small town spread thin like a film of dirt stretched across the country. They grew up with each other, or they went on jobs with each other, or they served time together.

But what it meant to a cop. Al Walsh met him at the little park near the subway entrance on West Seventy-second Street and gave it all to him.

Three days after the big jewel job in Boston he picked up two of the men. On his tip the Philadelphia police caught the rest and found the diamonds in back of a used car dealer's office where Otto Fantastic was splitting them down for a quick resale.

Two hours after the teletype said the Jersey State Police had found the mutilated body of Nickie Real he picked Looie Katz and a redhead up at the airport getting on a plane for Mexico.

The neighborhood called him a straight, smart cop who was going up. The boys at the station house called him Miracle-man Milazzo.

Then one day Al Walsh came to the park with a hot special. The guy they tried to heist last night—the one where they slammed the door on the guy's fingers to make him tell where the extra cash was; and when he wouldn't talk they banged him over the head with the tail end of a gun until his screams woke up the neighborhood. Well, one of the guys on that caper was Rocky Tosco. And not alone either. That blonde bitch Millie who got her kicks watching guys getting beaten up had been along too. They had pushed the attendant up against a barbed-wire fence and Rocky had beaten him with the gun until the guy had passed out.

When he heard the name he must have jumped ten feet. He wasn't on duty, but he didn't care. To pinch Rocky he'd come back from the grave.

He found the punk in bed. Cocky Rocky. With that stinking grin on his face.

"You got the wrong guy, Detective."

He didn't answer. He just looked around. On the dresser he found the two stubs. One for a suit at the dry cleaners, the other for shirts at the laundry. Both dated that morning.

"Okay, Rocky," he said. "You got two minutes to dress, or I'll take you as you are."

Rocky moved fast. But he still had to tie his shoe laces and finish buttoning his shirt in the car. The first stop was the cleaners. The suit hadn't gone out yet. It was tied in a knot at the bottom of the basket. He looked it over and there were stains on the sleeve. He got the shirts in time too. One cuff had an edge of red. Blood. Rocky wasn't looking so good.

He dropped the stuff off at the lab for a workout. Then he took Rocky to the hospital.

"That's one of them," the gas station guy said through his bandages. "He's the one who kept slamming the door while the other held my hand. They were sore because there was only seventeen dollars in the cash drawer. I kept telling them my partner had just made a night deposit. Then this one started to hit me on the head with his gun."

Then he took Rocky up to the Bronx where the woman motorist lived. She had just pulled into the station for gas when the punks piled into their car and took off.

"Yes," she said. "I'm sure. This man was the last one into the car. He had a gun in his hand. He was just a few feet away. I couldn't be mistaken. That's the same man."

Back at the station house Rocky wanted his lawyer.

"You'll get your lawyer. But first tell us who the other two guys were."

"You're crazy. I wasn't in on that."

"Then the gasoline guy is crazy, and the dame from the Bronx is crazy too."

"Yeah. They're crazy too."

"And the stains on the suit? And the shirts?"

"I'm not talking."

"You don't have to, Rocky. The evidence speaks for itself."

"It's a lie. I want my lawyer."

"Who were your pals?"

"I want my lawyer."

"Did you guys pull that job on the liquor store on Ninety-sixth Street?"

"No."

"Did your gang take the delicatessen store in the Village last Thursday?"

"No."

"Then this was your first job?"

"No."

"What were the others?"

"There weren't any others."

"You just said there were."

"I didn't. I didn't. I want my lawyer."

After four hours he turned Rocky over to Harry Frank. Harry was a good cop but he had a heavy hand.

"Don't hit him where it shows, Harry."

Harry just laughed and went to work.

When he came back two hours later Rocky looked sick.

His shirt was ripped and his face was puffed. There was a bloody split on his lip that went up to his nostril.

"That was stupid," he told Harry.

"Look, no son of a bitch is going to call me a son of a bitch."

"Okay. I'll take over."

He let Rocky read the lab reports. The stains on his suit were blood. The stuff on his shirt was blood—the same type of blood that oozed out of the gasoline guy's head.

"I want my lawyer."

"Give us a statement. We'll give you the phone."

Six hours later Rocky finally gave in.

Getting that statement signed was a big moment in his life. Now he had the proof. Now Gina would see that he was right. She'd never have anything to do with Rocky again.

His landlady banging away at his door woke him up. There was a call for him. He went out into the hall and answered the phone. It was the desk sergeant telling him to get down to the station quick.

All the way there he had happy dreams. It was probably the newspapers. Or maybe some big-shots from the mayor's office to give him a citation. But he was so wrong.

Only the captain was waiting. And he was mad.

"Milazzo, I thought you were one of the smart ones."

"What's up?"

"Your tail is up. And it's being roasted. Sit down."

He sat down and looked at the captain's face. It was almost purple with anger.

"I'm throwing your Rocky Tosco case out."

"You're what?" He jumped up.

"Sit down, Milazzo. I'm throwing it out to save you lots of trouble. But more important, to save the department from getting a black eye. When will you guys out there learn there's more to this business than getting a confession."

"I don't get it."

"Rocky Tosco's lawyer was here. Showed me a set of pictures. Rocky took four stitches in his lip. He also had a statement from doctors to prove Rocky confessed under physical duress."

"Aw, nuts. That old gag. Listen. The confession was on the level. I have two eyewitnesses. Blood-stain tests from the lab. What more do you want?"

"Shut up, Milazzo. It's not what I want. It's what the district attorney wants. It's what the judge wants. And most important of all it's what the jury wants."

"Look, Captain. All those punks cry their confession was beaten out of them. It's the stalest gag in the shyster's book. No jury will fall for it."

"Rocky's jury will fall for it, because Rocky's lawyer has a new angle to play. If we push the case the lawyer is going to twist it in our back. The newspapers will eat it up. I can just see the headlines." The captain pressed his hands against his forehead. "They give me the creeps."

"What are you talking about?"

"How the newspapers would play it. Sadist Cop Beats Fake Confession Out of Love Rival."

"What?"

"You know a girl named Gina Rossi?"

"Yeah."

"Well, this lawyer says you're trying to frame Rocky. This lawyer says he has a hundred witnesses who'll swear Rocky Tosco has been sleeping with your girl."

"That's a lie."

"Shut up, Milazzo. When a cop is personally involved in a case he should turn it over to another cop. You know that."

He got up and slammed out of the office, but the captain's words followed him. A hundred witnesses. Everybody knew about it but him. Gina Rossi was sleeping with Rocky Tosco.

Getting drunk was easy. But staying drunk, so drunk nothing hurt, that was a trick he couldn't learn. He gave up trying and took a fling at the horses. In a few weeks he owed the local shylock four hundred bucks, and it didn't help. There was only one thing left—women.

The moment he was off duty he went on the prowl, looking into the bars, standing around dancehalls, walking the streets. Always thinking that maybe the next one was the right one. The one who would help him forget.

He found plenty of frumps on a fling, and oversexed bags looking for a bed, or just kids looking for romance.

They'd last an hour, a day. Soon it was over and he was on the prowl again.

He remembered the little Hanover woman. Sweet and abused. The first time he saw her was in the hall of the rooming house where he lived. She was using the phone. As he passed he could hear her speaking. Quiet and refined. She was wearing a neat tweed suit and very little make-up. A small, thin woman. But lots of dignity.

"Who's your new tenant?" he asked the landlady.

"Mrs. Hanover. Ain't she the jewel?"

"Mrs.? Then she's married."

"Bad luck for her. The husband is a heel."

Married, he thought. All the nice ones must be married.

He found himself meeting Mrs. Hanover in the hall quite often. She was polite, but cool. And that was the way he left it. Yet it couldn't stop him from thinking how lucky a guy could be going home every night and finding a wife like Mrs. Hanover waiting for him.

Then one afternoon she knocked on his door. She was wearing a neat pink housedress that was buttoned high at the neck and her eyes were red.

Could she talk to him? She had to talk to someone or

go mad.

He asked her to sit down and offered her a drink, but she refused. She only wanted to talk. She didn't have any friends in town, and she was at her wit's end.

It was about her husband. The story she told made him wince. The guy sounded like a combination of Dracula and Jack the Ripper. A couple of times he found himself wanting to kill the guy.

Mrs. Hanover reached into her pocket for a handkerchief and somehow while she wiped her eyes the button that held the pink dress together at her neck came undone. She was so busy drying her eyes she didn't notice it.

Then she started talking again. Every time she moved the damn neckline went lower. Soon she was showing an awful lot of breast, and for a small woman she had an awful lot of breast to show.

He kept figuring it was one of those embarrassing accidents. But he was only human.

"You sure you don't want a drink, Mrs. Hanover?"

"I'm sure."

"Then I'll get one for myself."

He got up and went over to the desk where he kept his bottle. He turned his back hoping she'd realize and fix herself up.

"Vincent."

He turned and she was standing right behind him. He looked down and she was still wide open.

"Vince," she said. "You don't know what it's like, living without love."

He put his drink down and stopped kidding himself. Every few days after that the refined little Mrs. Hanover would slink down the stairs to scratch at his door. Just like a cat. Then when it was over she pulled his arm around her, lay her head on his chest and complained about how her husband abused her.

In a week he had enough. He stopped letting her in. He just sat there in the dark and listened to her scratch at his door. After a while she caught on and left him alone. She probably found another door to scratch. Another ear to complain in.

Then there was the little farm girl. He found her down near Times Square gawking at the sights. She was nineteen, freckled and spending two weeks with her aunt in New Jersey. She lived in Deepwater, Nebraska. Population, two hundred and four. And wasn't New York thrilling?

The excited way she talked. The look in her eyes. The kick she got out of everything she saw. It made him laugh. He took her to the top of the Empire State Building. He rode the buses with her. Then walked her down Fifth Avenue.

The girl had magic. Showing her things made him see New York all over again. A fresh, exciting New York. He found himself explaining things he never realized he knew. Even the pushing crowds and murderous taxis became a joke.

He took her to a small side street restaurant and she kept asking him to point out the famous folks. He told her famous folks didn't eat there but she wouldn't believe it.

When the lights went on he took her up Broadway and she seemed to be in a dream. The funniest things sent her off—a stage door, or a fancy dame wrapped in a Pekinese and a mink, or some musicians in tuxedos lugging their instruments into a drug store.

Watching her face he could understand why old men of sixty sometimes married girls of fifteen. It was like getting a second mortgage on youth. Sort of sitting back and free-loading on someone else's innocence.

It had been a wonderful day. But it was getting late.

A couple of times he asked when she had to get the bus

to her aunt's house in Jersey but she always changed the subject.

By twelve-thirty he felt like his feet were going to break through his shoes.

"I guess you've seen everything."

"No. I haven't seen the parks."

"Parks? Not in New York. Not at night. They're dangerous."

"Who for?" she giggled. "The boys? Or the girls?"

He took another look at her. A million freckles. A shining nose. Deepwater, Nebraska. Maybe he had a dirty mind. Maybe she really wanted to see the park.

They took a cab to Riverside Drive. And as they walked along the path her hand worked its way into his. It was a hot little hand.

Then suddenly in a dark turn she stopped.

"I want to thank you."

"Sure."

But that was all he got a chance to say. Her hard body hit him. She reached up and pulled his head down and she pressed her mouth against his lips so tight they spread. Then she gave him a dose of tongue that almost fractured his tonsils.

It all happened about four feet from the path. Every now and then he thought he heard people passing. But one thing he was sure of. The kid was from the country. The damp grass. The hard earth. The sharp bushes. No city girl could have taken that kind of beating and had so much fun.

In fact when she came to see him on the days that followed they went to his room. But on a bed it was never so wild, never so exciting, and he was glad when her vacation was over and the little freckled hick packed up her tongue and body and went back to service the town of Deepwater.

Sometimes he was convinced there was no such thing as a good woman. Then he met the high-school teacher. She really rocked him. She was the worst of the lot. But in a way she cured him.

He picked her up in the park one day. She must have been ten years older than he was. And she was tall. Even in her low heels she came up to his ear. A colorless woman who wore her pale blonde hair in a knot on the back of her neck. But she was smart and it was nice talking to her.

They sat near the lake and watched the boats. They walked along looking at squirrels and laughing at the fresh pigeons. She asked a lot of questions about his work, about the Department, and his future. The direct way she asked made him think a little of Gina Rossi.

Then it started to drizzle. By the time he caught an empty cab they were wet.

"Let's go to my place," she said, "so I can change into something dry."

Her place was a large room. There was a kitchen behind a screen. A bay window that looked out over the wet street. Soft chairs and frilly lamps. A nice warm room.

"Turn your back," she said.

He heard the closet door open. He heard the rustling sound of silky things and then the closet door closed.

"Now," she said.

He turned around and looked. Her blonde hair was loose and hung over her shoulders in long soft waves. She was wearing a white thing that went down to her bare pink toes. It was pulled tight around her middle by a wide white leather belt that was full of copper nail heads.

"Take your wet jacket off," she said, "and I'll make some hot coffee."

He laid his jacket across the back of a chair, then sat down to watch her. Every time she stepped in front of the light he could see the black shadow of her body through the white thing she was wearing. It was a good, full body and he wondered why he hadn't noticed it in the park.

They sat on the couch and drank coffee. She kept asking him questions about his family, about Italian people. She even asked about his love life. As he talked he noticed how fine and young her white skin was.

"And then what about Gina?" she asked.

He told her. Getting it off his chest made him feel better. And he kept wondering why he ever thought this woman was old. Right now she looked like a young girl in a white confirmation dress. The only thing that spoiled the picture was her eyes. They had a cloudy look he couldn't understand.

He had talked about himself for over an hour when she laughed.

"Vince," she said. "I've figured you out."

"Tell me. I'd like to know too."

"You're a horseman on a crusade. A knight with a rubber lance."

"Break that down to something a little more simple."

"You go from experience to experience looking for a virtuous woman, a saint you can enshrine in your bedroom, a girl with a built-in chastity belt."

"You aren't making much sense."

"Vince." Her laugh was full of meanness. "I have bad news for you. The girl you're looking for doesn't exist. Women aren't saints. They're animals."

She was leaning so close he could feel the warmth of her body and the couch seemed to shake with her intensity.

"Vince, women don't want respect. They don't want to be kept on a pedestal. That's a false veneer. Down deep they all want to be dominated. To be dragged by the hair into a cave and ravished."

"Yeah," he tried to smile. "But I haven't got a cave."

"Vince," she took him by the shoulders and drew him even closer. "A woman wants to be crushed. She wants her bones to be ground into powder. Humiliated and dominated."

He put his arms around her and tried to kiss her but she pulled away and jumped to her feet. Now she looked like a mean, golden lioness.

"You were going to kiss me," she accused him.

"Is that bad?"

"What a stupid way to make love."

"Take it easy." He was getting mad. "Give me a chance."

The cloud was gone from her eyes. Now they were full of sparks—red, ugly sparks.

"You look like a man. You've got the shoulders. You're good looking. But you want to make love without mussing your hair. You're all the same."

He was beginning to see red. "What kind of a crack is that?"

She leaned close and laughed in his face.

"I'll tell you something else you won't like," she was whispering now. "You made a slut of Gina."

"What!"

"For years she waited. All you had to do was give her some encouragement and she would have waited longer. But not you—you were too noble. You had to do the right thing."

What was he taking this for? He got up and started for his jacket.

"Run, Vince," she sang out. "Run from the truth. Run, little wop."

"Shut up!" he hollered, and banged his fists together.

"You drove Gina right into Rocky's bed."

Then he slapped her. Right across the mouth. But it didn't stop her. She just laughed at him.

"Is that the best you can do?"

Quickly her fingers undid her belt. Then she shook out of the white thing and stood in front of him, naked.

"Stop being a gentleman," she said.

She pressed the wide leather belt with the copper nail heads into his hand.

"Be an animal."

He struck her across the legs and she went down on her knees laughing at him. He hit her across the back and she rolled over on the floor.

All the crazy hate of all the crazy lonely nights came out. He hit for Gina. He hit for Rocky. He hit until the white body on the floor was red.

And she rolled there until the laugh became a happy whimper and then a sigh. But he didn't stop hitting until she crawled to his feet and laid her cheek against his shoe. Then he snapped out of it.

What the hell was he doing? He dropped the belt, grabbed his jacket and ran out of the place.

He walked the wet streets for hours. The cooling rain washed his face. It soaked his clothes and ran down his body. But he still felt dirty and scared.

He had to get hold of himself. If he kept leading this kind of life he'd wind up on the police line-up with the rest of the sex perverts. And the terrible part was that some of the things the crazy schoolteacher said were true.

He had never asked Gina to wait. He had no right to be angry. But he couldn't help it. Even now, after all these years, he was still bitter about Gina and Rocky.

It was a long time since the captain gave him the lecture. Four years. By now he was Detective First Grade.

Al Walsh the gambler was dead. Someone found out he was a stoolie and they played tit-tat-toe on his body before shoving it out of a racing car.

Rocky was no longer a punk stick-up man. He was a big-time restaurant owner. A guy who had worked his way through Gina and plenty of other women.

And Gina Rossi! He was standing in front of her house the day before Christmas waiting to arrest her brother for murder.

Gina. Why did she do it with Rocky? Any other guy in the world, and he wouldn't care. But with Rocky Tosco. And the whole neighborhood knowing. That he couldn't take.

He finally saw her coming down the street toward him. She worked in a Fifth Avenue music shop, but she looked more like the cover off a fashion magazine—tall, graceful, long-legged.

She was wearing a gray coat that was belted tight around her slim waist and swung out full at the skirt. She carried it like mink, and the stand-up collar framed her face like a petal around a bud. As she got closer he could see the large dark eyes, the fine nose and the full warm mouth.

She was as beautiful as all his dreams.

She saw him standing there, and for a second he felt the hesitation in her flowing walk. But then she came on without the slightest change of expression.

She walked right up to him.

"What do you want, Vincent?"

That was Gina. Direct. She never ran from anything.

"Where's Pete?"

"I won't tell you."

She turned and started into the house.

"Gina. I have to talk to you."

"Then come upstairs. It's too cold out here."

"Your mother's upstairs. I'd rather not worry her. Let's go someplace else."

"Where?"

The big round clock in front of the jeweler's said it was almost twelve. Six hours since he stared at Tony Statella's body. He wasn't hungry. But he ought to eat. And it would be a place to talk to Gina.

"How about a restaurant?"

"I couldn't eat."

"A cup of coffee?"

"All right."

The moment she agreed he got a funny feeling. There was the collection they took up for the widow. And that five-spot he gave to the Orphans' Christmas Fund. The few presents he bought. And just before he had shelled out ten dollars to Money-mad Minetta. There wasn't more than two bucks in his wallet.

As they walked he put his hand in his pocket and fished around trying to figure how much change he had. It felt like a quarter and a nickel. Big-shot Milazzo, asking a girl into a restaurant a couple of days before payday.

Then he saw the car up at the corner. Good old Whiteman. He felt like kissing the guy.

"Excuse me," he said. "I'll be right back. I have to check with my partner."

He hurried ahead and rapped on the window. Whiteman lowered it.

"What's new, Whiteman?"

"I squeezed some more pigeons for you, Vincent. All the stories check. A bricklayer killed Tony."

"What else?"

"I called Central and the hatcheck girl is still picture-gazing. If the story is on the level and this bricklayer hasn't got a police record she won't find anything. I heard something else. Tony was in on some long distance deals. He was doing business with Sassy Beckwith from New Orleans."

"The guy who has those tourist traps near Bourbon Street?"

"The same. The other deal was with Richard Cross."

"I don't know him."

"Sure you do. He's society—owns a string of hotels. Your boy, Tony, was traveling around in a mixed crowd."

"You keep digging, Whiteman. I'm working on another lead."

"Some lead. I saw you talking to her. If I wasn't married I'd swap two of my private pigeons for her."

"It's all business."

"Yeah, Vincent," his partner said sadly. "That's what's wrong with you. Any guy who can talk to a dame like that and only think of business is nuts. Go on, ask her for a date. I won't tell the captain you did it on the city's time."

"Stop horsing around. Keep digging. See what else you can find out about Tony. And Rocky too. I'll see you at the station house in an hour."

Whiteman started to run the window up.

"One more thing, Whiteman."

"Yeah."

"I'm short. Let me have twenty."

"Twenty! On Christmas week?" Whiteman pulled out his wallet and looked around in it. "Here's ten."

He shoved the bill in his pocket and stepped back as the car took off.

Gina was still waiting for him.

"Any special place?" he asked.

"No."

"Then let's get out of the neighborhood."

He took her arm and walked her over to a cab. He gave the driver the address of a small steak house off Fourteenth Street. Not too fancy, but clean and quiet.

He ordered a steak but Gina said she didn't want anything.

"Did you have breakfast?"

She shook her head.

"You've got to eat. I'm getting you a steak, too."

When the waiter left, he leaned back and looked at her. "Well, Gina, what have you decided to do?"

"I'm going to get my brother a lawyer. A smart criminal lawyer who can make arrangements. I've seen them do it for others. They can do it for Pete."

"Do you have fifty thousand dollars?"

"No."

"Then that kind of a lawyer won't even bother to talk to you."

"There must be some lawyer who'll help."

"A shyster will bleed you for what he can get. A good lawyer will tell you the same thing I will."

"What is that?"

"Your brother committed a crime. He's got to turn himself in."

"I can't give up that easily."

"Gina, right now your brother is hiding somewhere. He's a frightened kid. Instead of telling him to come out and take his medicine you promised to save him. But after he's been holed up a couple of days and you tell him you can't do a thing, your brother Pete's going to change. He's going to be afraid to come out and take it. Fear pulls that thin coat of civilization right off a guy, even a guy as nice as Pete. He'll become an animal, a killer. He'll do anything to get away. It won't be good for you or your mother. Or for Pete."

"Neither will the electric chair. No, Vincent. I've got to try and help Pete. A good lawyer and the truth will save him."

"And what's the truth, Gina?"

"Tony Statella deserved to die."

"Sure. I'll buy that. But Pete isn't God."

"No, but he had a reason. A good lawyer can explain that to a jury. Tony was blackmailing Pete's fiancée."

He couldn't look at her face. Those brown eyes were full of conviction. She was so sure she was right.

"You see," she went on. "Pete's been engaged to Marie three years. He was saving money to buy a home—that's why he worked at those high-paying jobs on government projects. He spent eighteen months on some islands in the Pacific and sent all his money home so Marie could put it in their account. The nine months in Alaska was to give them the rest of the money they needed."

Gina stopped talking to let the waiter lay out the spread and put the steaks on the table. He started to eat but Gina just stared at the food.

"Go ahead, eat," he said.

Her long graceful fingers picked up the knife and fork and then put them down.

"When Pete came home yesterday Marie cried and told him the entire story. She had been foolish enough to pose for some silly pictures. And Tony Statella was blackmailing her with them. Well, naturally, when Pete heard about it he went right to Tony and demanded the return of the pictures. You would have done the same."

"Yeah," he answered softly. "I know. But when Tony refused, Pete came back with a gun and killed him."

"How would you feel if someone took advantage of the girl you loved?"

That question hit home. He put his knife and fork down.

"Once something like that did happen to me. But I figured if a girl wanted to play in rough company she deserved to get hurt. So I didn't kill the guy." He was looking right at her. But Gina didn't seem to realize he was talking about her. "Your brother Pete was a fool. And Marie was a tramp."

"That's a terrible thing to say."

"Tony didn't twist Marie's arm to make her climb out of her clothes. She took them off herself. Right in front of a camera. So morons all over the country could drool. For me a girl like that is sick. Lower than a prostitute."

"You've been a policeman too long, Vince. For you there is no shading. Just black and white. I can't be that way. I talked to Marie this morning. I agree she was foolish. But not bad."

"This I got to hear. All my life I've wondered what went on in their little heads as they stripped in front of a camera. What's Marie's story?"

"It began a year ago at her cousin's birthday party. Marie has a sweet voice and they urged her to sing. When the party broke up this fellow asked to take her home. He told her she ought to be a singer, that with a few lessons she could probably find a good job and make money. Well, Marie is human. The idea of being a singer, of helping Pete with the money, sounded grand. She took the fellow's card. It had the address of a man who was a voice teacher."

"A guy named Alvin Allen?"

"That's right. He was supposed to be one of the best."

"The man's a swindler. He's so crooked he picks his own pockets."

"Marie didn't know that. She went to him, and he gave her an audition. He was enthused; he said with a few lessons he'd be able to get her a job with a Broadway musical."

"How much a lesson?"

"Ten dollars."

"That wasn't much."

"Well, five lessons a week ran into money. Marie was borrowing it all from the joint account. She was going to put it back the moment she began to work. But every time she questioned them about the job they promised she was told she wasn't quite ready."

"The bloodsuckers."

"When she had drawn five hundred dollars out she became panicky. She finally broke down and cried at the school. They refused to refund her money or give her a job, but they suggested she see Tony Statella. Tony was very kind. He said she could earn the money by modeling."

"But first she needed some professional pictures."

"Yes. How did you know?"

"I was a girl once."

"Still not convinced, are you, Vincent?"

"Oh, I can see how it would happen. I see stuff like that every day. So she posed for the nudes to get a set of professional pictures."

"The photographer told her they were artistic studies. They would only be released to professional artists and students to use for copying. He made it sound all very proper and dignified. And Marie wanted to return the money to the account before Pete came home."

"Stop the hearts and flowers."

"All right." She sighed. "When Tony saw the pictures he was very impressed. Marie is a lovely little girl. He told her he would introduce her to some men who would pay her five hundred dollars for one night. Marie said no."

"Hurrah for Marie. She's one in a million. You'd be surprised at how few say no."

"I'm not getting anywhere, Vincent. Nothing will change your mind. I think I'd better go."

"Look, Gina. I'm not a judge or a jury. I'm a cop. My job is to turn your brother in."

"Yes, you're a cop—a big, thickheaded cop." Her eyes were getting wet. "If you were such a wonderful cop you'd have arrested Tony Statella a long time ago so he wouldn't be around to hurt people like Marie and Pete."

"If it wasn't Tony it would be someone else. Girls like

Marie will always get into trouble. You can't stop them. Remember how I warned you about Rocky?"

"I don't see the comparison. Rocky asked me out and I went. He was a good date. He took me to the best shows and finest restaurants. And he was always respectful. A perfect gentleman."

"Then why didn't he marry you?"

"I was never in love with Rocky. I didn't want to marry him."

Well, that was her story. There was no use talking about it.

"Vincent, look at me." He looked up. "Do you know why I stopped seeing Rocky? Not because you told me to. But because we quarreled over you. Rocky said something I didn't like. He told me you were a man with an inferiority complex, that you became a cop so you could bully and push and feel big. The uniform and the authority gave you a feeling of importance."

"Big words for Rocky."

"The words are mine. The thought was Rocky's. I hated him for talking about you that way. I told him so. And I refused to go out with him again. But now I see he was right. You're not a man with a heart. You're a uniform full of hate."

"That's me. The man with the heavy hate."

She stood up to leave.

"Vincent," she said, her voice tired. "You manage to hurt me more than anyone else I know."

He couldn't let her go like this.

"Sit down, Gina. I want to say something."

She sat down. Her large dark eyes were full of waiting. But what could he say to her? Gina, I love you and want to marry you after I arrest your brother,

"Well, Vincent?"

He had to look away.

"Gina, you're the one person in the world I never want to hurt."

"What does that mean?"

"It means I'm going to do something for your brother."

"Oh, Vincent!" Her lip began to quiver.

"But understand—your brother killed a man. He just can't walk away free. He's got to pay something. I'll do my best to see that he gets a break. But keep him in line, and when I call, bring him."

She reached out and her fingers lightly touched his hand. "I knew you would help, Vincent."

He looked into her face.

"When this is over, Gina, I'm going to have something to say to you."

"I'll be waiting, Vincent," she said softly.

Then she got up and he watched her walk out.

Wonderful Gina.

Well, now he had to do something. Ever since he saw Rocky that morning there had been an idea. A mad, crazy idea. And he was going to use it.

The waiter dropped the check. Six dollars—and no one had even touched the steaks. He left a dollar tip and walked out.

The sky was almost black, and the air was wet. He looked at the change in his hand. Well, today was his day for doing crazy things. He might as well be broke as the way he was. Instead of a subway he flagged a cab and rode to the station house.

He nodded to the desk sergeant, took the turn to the right and went up the old wooden stairs. There wasn't much doing in the big room. Someone had nailed a Christmas wreath on the mustard-colored walls. Abraham Lincoln's picture was still hanging crooked and one of the steam radiators was whistling like a ruptured peanut stand.

The door to the chief's cubbyhole was open. He looked in and the old man was yes-sirring the telephone. When the chief saw him he motioned him in.

He squeezed between the two filing cabinets and sat down on the metal chair.

"Oh, certainly." The chief was smiling into the phone. "You've made it quite clear. And I agree."

That was the chief—a split personality. When he was talking up the line to big shots he was all smiles and sweetness. To get up that high in the department he had to lick toes.

But when he talked down to the men under him he was a heartless dog. There could be only one way to do things—his way. And giving him an excuse was as useless as talking to the pile of department directives on his desk.

And this was the man he was going to try and swing a deal with. He realized more than ever how crazy his idea was.

"Ha!" The old man laughed into the phone. "That's very good."

He was a dapper guy with a head full of silver hair. He looked like the conductor of a classy symphony orchestra.

"Thanks for calling. No! No! Never too busy to talk to you. 'Bye now."

He slammed the phone down and the smile became a scowl.

"The newspapers are having trouble, Milazzo. Christmas season. No international news breaking. Washington is closed for the holidays. No news coming out of City Hall. So they've decided to whip up circulation by crucifying the police department. That can't miss. Nobody likes a cop. When they start to holler the police are crooked, every woman who's been bawled out for jay-walking, every guy who's gotten a ticket for overtime parking jumps on the bandwagon. It must sell papers. Otherwise they wouldn't do it so often."

The chief stopped talking to stare out the door. His face was getting very red. Suddenly he jumped up and leaned over his desk.

"Who the hell," he shouted, "is whistling out there?"

The whole office went dead. Except the shrill sound of the whistle. Then one of the boys called in.

"It's the valve on the steam radiator."

"Get it fixed," the chief said. "It's driving me out of my mind."

"We called maintenance three hours ago."

"Call them again. And then again. Get it fixed." He sat down and looked at the phone. "Milazzo, you're handling the Statella killing yourself. I'm glad. I've seen you do some good work. If the department ever needed a rabbit pulled out of a hat it's now. The City Hall Cadets feel the newspapers may blow this up into a club to swing at the administration next election."

"That's a long time off."

"The newsboys will keep it up as long as it sells newspapers. City Hall wants it stopped at any price, so they can stay in power. No one cares how many cops go under. And that's the story. Orders are to break something in twenty-four hours or face a shakeup."

"A shakeup?"

"Yeah." The old man sighed. Then the buzzer on his desk rang and he jerked up the phone.

"Who?" he growled. "What the hell does he want? No! No! Put him on." The smile came back. The voice became friendly. "Yes, sir. Of course. You're absolutely right."

He stopped listening. He was thinking about what the chief had said. A shakeup. That was bad.

Public opinion was an emotional thing that couldn't be

reasoned with.

"I was standing on the corner," an angry letter to a newspaper would say. "The light was in my favor and I started across. Then this car comes down at me doing at least fifty miles an hour. Right through the red light. Why do the police allow this?" Go ahead and explain that there are over thirty thousand intersections in New York City. And over a hundred thousand motorists who didn't deserve a license.

"My car was stolen," a man tells the desk sergeant. "And there was a cop standing right around the corner. Is that what I pay taxes for?" Try and tell him there are over a hundred and twenty thousand corners in the city for a cop to be around when something happens. Or try and tell him it was his own fault for leaving the keys in his car.

"My little boy," a hysterical mother screams. "Killed while crossing the street. Why do you police let it happen?" How could you point out that the city streets if untangled and laid straight would reach from California to London. Or that if she taught her kid not to jaywalk he might still be alive.

"I was walking by the river," a crying girl tells the reporters. "And this man drags me behind a building. I screamed and screamed but no police came."

The papers spread it big. But they forget to tell that the girl was a little high, and that she had just picked the fellow up at a bar. They also forget to tell their readers that New York City's waterfront is over five hundred and seventy-five miles long—the distance from New York to Detroit. All darkness and docks.

Then there were the parks, and parades, and opening nights. Diplomats getting off planes, movie stars getting off trains. Everyone wanted police protection from a handful of cops—cops who made a little more money than a garbage collector. Cops who had to climb out on a window ledge after a would-be suicide, or scale a wall to save a cat, or charge into a dark alley where hopped-up punks were waiting with itchy guns.

But there wasn't any use in trying to tell that side of the story. When the pressure was on, the only thing to do was tell the public they were right. The police department was wrong and they were going to have a shakeup to straighten things out.

Like every group of men, the police department had its bad apples. There were some crooks, but they were kicked out the minute they were caught—except for those who were too strong with political connections. And even they only lasted as long as their connection. Then they went. There were sadistic cops, but the moment they showed their colors they were pushed out.

So all a department shakeup ever got was a few poor monkeys who had used bad judgment, or made a bum decision. They were the ones selected as victims.

They got a trial. The papers got their headlines. The public got its revenge. Cops were kicked out, detectives busted, transfers made. And then a statement was issued: the shakeup was over; the police department had been properly punished.

The chief finished his call and slammed the receiver down. He pulled out a handkerchief and wiped his forehead. Then suddenly he jumped up.

"That whistle," he shouted. "What the hell are you doing about that whistle?"

There was a moment of silence, and then a terrible metallic bang. The chief looked at him a second, then sat down.

"Milazzo," he said softly. "Go out and see what they've done."

He pushed between the filing cabinets and looked into

the big room. One of the men was standing in front of the radiator with a hammer in his hand. The valve was lying on the floor and a thick cloud of steam and hot water was oozing out. But there was no more whistle. The guy with the hammer winked at him and he had to laugh.

He went back into the cubbyhole and sat down.

"They just took the whistle out of the radiator."

"About time." The chief went back to his chair, and then the sour look came to his face and he leaned forward again. "A shakeup! Milazzo, you know what that means?"

"I know."

"That's why we've got to crack the Statella case."

"I know who killed Tony."

"You do?" The chief looked at him. "You do!" It was a shout. "Why in hell didn't you say so?" His hand went out for the phone.

"But I can't make the arrest."

The hand came away from the phone.

"Why not?"

"Because the guy who killed Tony isn't important. He's just a young kid who got mixed up. He doesn't deserve to take a full rap."

"Milazzo! Milazzo! You're not King Solomon. You're a cop. Arrest the guy."

"Look, Chief, I stumbled on something so big and so dirty even the newspapers will be happy. It will hit the town like an H-bomb. And it will cross the country too. The hardest thing to hit the underworld since they developed the fingerprint."

"Sure. Sure, that's great. But in the meantime bring in the Statella killer so I can get the papers off our tail."

"No."

"No?" The old man looked like he wasn't hearing right.

"I can't. The kid being free is my whole case."

"Is the kid a stoolie?"

"No. But me acting like I'm looking for Statella's killer will give me the leverage I need."

The chief wiped his forehead. Then he smiled. He was talking real nice now. Like to the Chief Inspector, or the Commissioner,

"Milazzo, you've been seeing too many movies. Things like this don't happen in real life. Forget your one-man reform ticket. Just bring me the killer."

"No."

The chief banged the desk so hard a pile of directives fell to the floor.

"Look, Chief," he said before the old man could start to talk. "I'm on to something big. It's a syndicate that's got its meter on the rump of every fast dame in town— prostitution, white slavery, Mann Act violations and black-mail. I've got the names, and in three weeks I can have the evidence."

"Three weeks! Listen, Milazzo, you give me that killer right now. In half an hour I can satisfy City Hall and the newspapers, and all the cops under me can enjoy a peaceful Christmas without sweating out the thought of a shakeup."

"I want three weeks and protection."

"Protection?"

"Yeah. I want you to cover for me when complaints start coming in about Milazzo being out of line—that Milazzo is playing rough. I want you to forget the calls. I'll need a free rein."

"Now I know you're crazy. Listen, Milazzo, you're a detective. You do your work, behave yourself and you got a good job. Plenty of security and no responsibility. No one to take crap from but me. And if you don't like your job you can quit. You're young yet, and you can start over, but not me. I've beat my brains out to get where I am. And what have I got? A job where every two-bit politician and ticket fixer can tell me off. I'm the buffer between the department and the public. Every cop under me is out to steal my job, and every guy above me is kicking me in the face so I won't take his job. Well, I'm tired of it. The only reason I'm hanging on is because in two years I retire, with a stinking pension and a bullet scar on my hip. That's what I've got to show for thirty years of hell. And if you think I'm going to climb out on a limb and jeopardize that pension just to let you go cowboying around town, you're crazy."

Was that the whole story? He'd worked under this man a long time, but what did he really know about him? What did he know about his partner, Whiteman, or anyone else on the force?

There were stoolies right in the police department, cops who turned reports over to politicians so they could raise hell in the election, who sold scandal to the newspapers, who ratted on other cops in order to get promotions. The Commissioner had his own gestapo squad, specially picked stooges who roamed the streets looking for trouble, spies who worked in the departments looking for trouble. Any trouble, just so they could fill out a report. The mayor had his rats, and the district attorney had his friends.

And besides all the informers, there were the cops who sold information to the crooks. They sent out tips on plans for a raid or arrest. They tipped lawyers off on what kind of evidence there was, trying to pick up a few extra bucks. The department was full of them. One of the first things a cop learned was never to trust anyone—especially a cop.

What did he know about the chief? Maybe he was a key man in the syndicate. Maybe he was their cover man. Well, now was the time to find out. There was little more he could lose.

"Chief," he asked, "what do you think of Detective

Scotti of Division?"

"Scotti? He's good. If I had ten more men like him I could send the rest of you out to watch parades."

Another knot in the string. He was pretty sure now why the chief wasn't interested in his proposition. There had probably been a phone call already saying Milazzo was stepping on toes.

"If Scotti is so good, how come he has an after-hour joint running wide open in his territory?"

The Chief leaned back and slowly mopped his head again. "Milazzo, what are you getting at?"

"I figure a joint like that shells out a thousand a week to stay open."

"So?"

"I was wondering who Scotti splits the dough with."

The old man's face got red, so red he expected to see blood squirt out of his ears. But instead he suddenly sighed and leaned back in his chair.

"Milazzo, you used to be a good cop, but lately you have lost your sense of humor. A cop without humor is no good."

"Maybe I don't see anything to laugh at."

"I know what you're trying to say about me and I'm laughing. In fact I'm going to take time out to tell you a funny story."

"About Detective Scotti and Rocky?"

"Get up and shut the door. Then sit down and shut your mouth."

When he was sitting down again he lit his pipe and listened.

"This happened—" the chief was smiling—"in the twenties—prohibition, Al Capone, and me a young detective in Brooklyn. One night I hear this noise in a rough dive near Sands Street. I shove through the laughing crowd. In the middle is a fight. Some guy has taken the gun from a cop and is beating the buttons off him. Well, I couldn't let that happen. If the hood got away with it, next to the Dodgers, beating up cops would become the big Brooklyn pastime."

There was a happy look of remembering in the chief's eyes.

"I was young then," he said. "A happy-go-lucky detective like you. I took off the jacket and the gun and handed it to my partner. Then I went in, right in front of his friends and the whole neighborhood. I murdered him. It was beautiful. When the guy was a bloody pulp on the floor I grabbed a handful of his hair and pulled him to his feet. Then in front of all that scum I walked the cop-beater right smack into the wall. He lost four of his front teeth."

The chief chuckled and shook his head sadly.

"Good old days," he said. "When I got the tough guy back to the station house some of the other boys took over. We were rough on rats in those days. We used a rubber hose instead of psychology. And it paid off."

The chief thought for a moment and then slowly the smile left his face.

"You can imagine how I felt when I got in the next day and someone had sprung the hood. He was out—free and clean. I asked everyone how come, but no one knew a thing. A month later I get a call someone is breaking up a restaurant. Who do you think it is?"

"Your rough friend?"

"Right. I rush him back to the station house all set to give him a workout but there's telephone call waiting for me. Orders from the Commissioner. Don't touch the guy. The next morning he's sprung. Six months later three punks are blindfolded, gagged and walked off the edge of a ten-story roof. I get a tip from a stoolie on who did it."

"Your rough friend."

"The same. I start to make the pinch but word comes down for me to lay off. I'm dizzy. Nothing makes sense."

The chief laughed.

"Well, next thing I hear my friend has gone to Chicago and made good. He's a big wheel with Al Capone's butchers. Then a year later Al Capone is caught on an income tax rap—a great day in American history."

The old man leaned forward over the desk.

"But this is the inside dope. Do you know who found out where the books were? The real books and not the dummies?"

"Your rough friend."

"Right. The guy was an undercover agent. He was sent to Brooklyn to build himself a reputation for being a tough guy. Beating the cop up was a gag. Being sprung was fixed. And killing three useless punks was strong stuff. But it worked, because when he got to Chicago Al had heard of him and was glad to get a guy like that on his crew."

The chief laughed.

"An undercover man! And I knocked out four of the poor guy's teeth. You can see how stupid I felt."

"Are you trying to tell me Rocky Tosco is a Federal Agent?"

"Hell, no. I'm just telling you that when you're a cop you don't have the right to ask questions, or to jump to any conclusions. You just walk straight without looking right or left. No matter what happens on either side you just keep walking straight."

"To hell with that." He got up so fast the hard metal chair tipped over. He didn't even bother to pick it up.

"Milazzo." The smile was gone. "You're a good cop. That's why I'm taking this much lip from you. But you've pushed far enough. Tony Statella was killed at six o'clock this morning. I want that killer brought in here and booked

by six tomorrow morning or you'll be a sad guy. I'm
going to bust you to pieces, and then I'm going to bust
the pieces. Now get out."

He got out. He was so sore he took the stairs down two
at a time and Whiteman hurried after him.

He got into the car and Whiteman stepped in behind
the wheel.

"Where to, happy boy?" his partner asked.

"I've got to see someone in the district attorney's office."

Whiteman started the car and they began moving
through the heavy traffic.

One department store had a great big laughing Santa
Claus in its window. He was nodding his head and rubbing
his belly while music came out of a loud speaker. People
with packages were going by. And a drunk was sitting on
the curb hugging his bottle.

What a stinking Christmas this was.

"Whiteman, who do you know in the D.A.'s office that
I can make a deal with?"

"What kind of a deal?"

"An honest one."

"Well," Whiteman said after he thought a while, "if I
were you I'd pick Jimmy Bell."

"Why?"

"He's as straight as you find them. He's high enough to
swing some weight, but low enough to be ambitious. Besides, he's Italian."

He felt the blood go to his head.

"What's that got to do with it?"

"Simple," Whiteman said. "When you need something
go to your own kind. That's what I'd do. You get more
understanding."

He wanted to hate Whiteman, but the guy was making
sense. Any decent guy would be able to understand what

Pete did. Understand why he blew his top when he found out how his girl was being shoved around. But an Italian would feel it more. And on a deal like he was trying to cook he had to use every angle. So he'd go to Jimmy Bell.

Whiteman pulled the car around back of the building, but he didn't get out.

"You better come up with me. I might be a long time."

"I'll wait down here," his partner said. "I don't like lawyers."

He took the elevator up and the girl at the desk told him he'd have to wait. He tried to lose himself in an old magazine but it didn't work. His mind was racing. The twenty minutes seemed like twenty years. But finally Bell came out and sized him up.

"Yes?"

He was a cold-looking blond guy with blue eyes.

"I'm Milazzo from Homicide. I'd like to talk to you."

The guy let it be seen he wasn't happy about his time being taken up. But he led him to a small partitioned square that was supposed to be an office.

Bell sat down behind his paper-loaded desk and lit a pipe. He took his own out and started it up.

"Don't get too comfortable, Detective. I'm in a hurry."

Now he was sure. He didn't like Bell. The guy was wearing his college education out loud so everyone could see he was one of the cultured kind. In fact his talk had a faint clipped accent that smelled of Boston.

"I've heard you're an honest lawyer, Bell."

"Detective Milazzo, in the practice of law honesty is no virtue. It's usually a sign of stupidity."

"I understand. You see, I'm stupid that way myself."

"Well, congratulations."

"Look." He pulled the pipe from his mouth. "I'll come right to the point."

"I'd appreciate that."

"I know a young boy, a nice kid who lost his head and killed a rat who deserved to die. One of those crazy things. And I don't want the kid to get hit with the whole book."

"Good day, Detective."

"Look, Bell."

"No, Milazzo. You look. Every day this office is full of weeping mothers and relatives, all trying to tell me their little boy is a good boy—just misunderstood. Do you know what I say?" His voice was as cold as his blue eyes. "I say, good day, Detective Milazzo."

His hand grew hard and tight around his pipe.

"Don't brush me, Bell. And don't try and freeze me. This kid has a legitimate beef. He found his girl was tricked into posing for some pictures. Any good Italian would know exactly how the kid felt."

"Is that why you came to me? Because I'm of Italian descent? Well, in this office we aren't Italian or Scandinavian or Zulus. Most of us are just fools who try to give the word justice some dignity. We try to give the law some meaning. Every time a shrewd shyster pokes a hole in it we rush forward like an army of ants and try to patch it up with saliva and good intentions. You came to see the wrong man."

"Fine speech, Bell. The kid is broke. So you'll push all the way and see that he gets the book. But if the same kid had fifty grand he could get a lawyer to make you and your whole office look like monkeys. That's your justice for you. Fifty-grand justice. Let's hear you speech out of that."

"Understand one thing." Bell didn't seem to have a temper. He was as cold as the wind blowing outside the window. "These unscrupulous lawyers you talk about have money to influence witnesses, and the money to locate new ones. They can even influence juries. But most important of all, time is always on their side. They study their case, calculate every angle, have their arguments and tricks all ready. They can do it. They take three or four cases a year. I have had to handle as many as twenty cases in one week. I can only devote three days to a case that needs months of preparation. That's why sometimes they can make us look like such bunglers. That's why we have what you so aptly call fifty-grand justice. It isn't our fault, or the ability of the shyster. It's because of an archaic system that overloads an undermanned office with more work than it can handle."

Bell moved the muscles of his mouth to make a smile.

"The defense rests, Detective." He said. "Now will you leave me to my work?"

"Bell, how would you like to put half the crooks in this city behind bars?"

"I'd love it. But Milazzo, knowing the crooks, even knowing what they are up to isn't important. I can go to any city in the country, talk to a few cab drivers, a few bellboys, a bartender or two. And when I'm done I'll know where every house of ill repute is, where every bookmaker and gambling game is, who dispenses narcotics, who disposes of stolen merchandise. That's the easy part. The difficult thing is the evidence."

"I'll give you enough evidence to smash a quarter of a billion dollar syndicate."

"I'm afraid that like most police officers, Milazzo, you don't have the slightest concept of what legal evidence really consists of. You see the law of our country has a subtle shading. In this office we're sworn to protect the individual from the state, and at the same time we're to protect society from the individual. It's rather complicated—too complicated for most policemen. I've seen them sitting in court groaning about how their beautiful perfect cases were being mishandled. On a few occasions I've been accused of selling out. Police officers are generally stupid about such things."

He wanted to get up and slap Bell across the mouth, not only to hurt him but to see if the guy really had blood. Instead he lit a match and held it to his pipe. When his hand stopped shaking he figured it was safe to start again.

"Bell, I know what evidence is. And I'll give you witnesses, too."

"Witnesses." Bell leaned back and carefully crossed a leg over his knee. "Dope addicts? Ex-convicts? Ex-patients from mental institutes? That's the kind of witnesses you police usually get me. Or an informer who will change his story for thirty cents. And even the honest witnesses—Mr. John Q. Public—how many times have they been intimidated or bought out?"

He was getting tired of the lecture. He poked the pipe into his pocket and stood up. He lay his hands on the desk and looked right into the guy's flat face.

"Look, Bell. Do you know the best kind of witness? A woman. A hurt, angry woman. When she decides to talk you can't stop her. Bullets, money, fear—nothing will stop her. She's going to talk."

"That's true, to an extent."

"True? Lucky Luciano was getting a percentage of every crime committed in the United States. On every sale of dope, every hot car, every robbery, some of the money fell into Lucky's pocket. Yet with all that against him the only thing they could pin on him was a charge of white slavery. Why? Because no one would talk until a smart young lawyer decided to play one prostitute against another. He worked them up. Rubbed their fur the wrong way and put them on the witness chair to spit. They spit Lucky right into jail. That's the kind of witnesses I'm offering you. Not one or two, but maybe a hundred. And the evidence?"

He reached into his jacket pocket, brought out the brown

envelopes and tossed them on Bell's desk.

Bell opened one up and studied the negatives.

"Sorry, Milazzo. These pictures aren't illegal. They don't show the wrong region."

"Notice the faces, Bell. The one you're looking at is a singer on television. That one there is in a show on Broadway. What does that smell like?"

"Blackmail."

"That's only the beginning. This thing stretches from Fort Wayne to Hollywood to New York. What does that smell like?"

"Mann Act."

"More. This syndicate is tied up with a big-time hotel chain, dives in New Orleans, and a hundred-thousand-dollar black book. This is what I'll do for you, Bell. I'll get you a list of the girls being blackmailed. I'll get a list of the girls shipped or coaxed across state lines. I'll get you a list of outlets. I'll get you the name of the top man, and I'll even try to get you the black book. Then you can build your own case. Subpoena your own witnesses. Get your own evidence."

"And in exchange for all this?"

"I want a kid to get a break. I want him to get as light a sentence as he deserves."

"That's quite a proposition. Quite a sales talk, too. But I can't commit myself on the strength of your promises."

"Bell, all I ask is that when I call you come running. And if I deliver what I promise you agree."

"That sounds fair enough."

"Where can I reach you if you aren't in your office?"

Bell wrote a telephone number on a memo pad, then ripped the sheet off and held it out. He took it and started for the door.

"Hey, Milazzo."

"Yeah."

"What part of Italy are your folks from?"

"Sicily."

"Sicilian, huh?" Bell nodded. "Then you may be able to do it."

He wanted to say go to hell, but instead he smiled and walked out.

As the elevator carried him down he felt good, even happy. Then he started across the big marble hall and he saw the clock. Ten after three. In less than fifteen hours he was supposed to book Tony Statella's killer or be broken.

In fifteen hours he had to work a miracle. What the hell did he have to feel happy about?

He slammed through the revolving doors and stepped out into the street. New York was getting its Christmas snow. Only it wasn't white and pretty like a picture on a calendar. It was wet and slushy and black. It looked just like his stinking future.

PART THREE

When he got into the car Whiteman started the motor. "Where now, Vince?"

That was a good question.

He needed information and lots of it. He needed someone who was a piece of a politician, someone who got around and whom people trusted—but someone who would talk as long as there was a set of ears willing to listen.

He smiled sadly. He knew a guy like that. He hadn't seen him in years because he couldn't stand his big mouth. But today, as much as he hated him, he needed the guy.

"There's an old Sicilian saying," he told his partner. "When you're in trouble turn to your family."

"So?" Whiteman asked.

"Let's go to Twenty-first and Tenth."

"What's there?"

"My Uncle Ralph."

It was an old firetrap of a building. Instead of waiting for the groaning elevator to come down, he took the worn wooden stairs up to the third floor loft.

Printed across the door was the name: Supreme Leather Works, Inc. Beneath it, in much bigger and fancier letters, Ralph Milazzo, President.

He turned the knob and shoved. A rusty bell hooked on the door clattered to let people know he was coming. But there weren't many people.

A couple of men played cards in a corner. Another man sat on a table eating a sandwich. The machines were all quiet and a heavy, lazy dust covered everything.

The only one working was a sloppy girl in a red smock. She was wrapping leather pencil cases in tissue paper and then boxing them. Her hands slowed down as her eyes took him in and when she smiled she showed a black space between her front teeth.

"Hello," she said.

"Mr. Milazzo in?" he asked.

"Sure. In the office." She tilted her head toward the front of the shop. "You looking for work?"

"No."

"You a salesman?"

He started toward the office.

"Hey!" she called. "What's the matter? You married or just stuck-up?"

The door to the office was marked Private, and then once again in big letters, Ralph Milazzo, President. He bounced his knuckles against the fancy lettering and his uncle called to come in.

The office was as dusty as the factory. There was a great

big old-fashioned green safe in the corner, sexy calendars on the walls, racing forms on the chairs, and behind the desk his uncle.

Every time he saw the man he got the same shock. His loudmouthed uncle looked exactly like his dead father—the same high forehead, the same warm blue eyes and the same slow smile. But what a difference in men!

His father had been loved and respected by everyone. His uncle was a small-time operator who tailed around after the big-shots and acted important. He fooled lots of people, but he was a phony.

"Come in," his uncle bellowed. "My favorite nephew."

"I'm your only nephew."

"True." His uncle smiled in that slow way that reminded him of his father. "But if I had a million nephews you'd still be my favorite."

At this point he usually told his uncle to cut the crap and they had an argument. But today he had to listen even if it turned his stomach.

His uncle took a bottle from the desk and poured liquor into a couple of paper cups. They wished each other a Merry Christmas and drank.

"Good stuff, nephew. Twelve-year-old bonded bourbon. Here, have a cigar." His uncle held out a box of fifty-centers. "Go ahead."

"I smoke a pipe."

"It's not a bribe. It's from an uncle."

He finally took one and slipped the cellophane off. His uncle unwrapped a cigar too and ran it back and forth under his nose.

"I love the smell of a good cigar and a bad woman," his uncle laughed. "Say, Vince, you never been to my new house. Nothing big. Just for your aunt and me. But it's got the best. A card room with a glass bar in the cellar. A two-car garage with magic eyes to open the doors."

While his uncle talked he wondered about the heavy silence that covered the factory.

"Business must be good," he finally said. "I see you even got a new safe."

"That." His uncle jerked a thumb toward the big green hulk. "I picked it up second-hand. I use it so nobody will borrow my liquor and cigars. But you're right, business is great. Just finished my best season last week."

That was a lie. It took more than a week for the machinery to catch all that dust. Yet the cuff links in his uncle's shirt sleeves looked like gold, and the tie he wore was a hand-blocked job costing at least twelve bucks.

That was his dirty cop mind. Always looking for trouble. He should know his Uncle Ralph was the biggest four-flusher in town.

He remembered back when he was a kid and his uncle came into the coffee shop on Saturdays. Uncle Ralph with pointy shoes and a gray suit, a dark shirt and a yellow tie held in place with a diamond stickpin. He talked for hours about the big people he did business with and the big deals he was closing. Then sooner or later he would see his uncle step into the back room and put the bite on his father. Five dollars to pay an electric bill or ten dollars for the doctor because one of the kids was sick.

When he got the loan Uncle Ralph went back to tell more stories as long as anyone would listen.

"Hey, Vince, I asked you a question."

"What?"

"Your aunt would like to see you. And your cousins too. Tony married a rich girl. Your cousin Anna is going with a boy who's loaded—real society. Why don't you spend tomorrow with us?"

Christmas Day with his gabby uncle and his spoiled cousins. That's all he needed.

"I can't, Uncle Ralph. I'm on duty."

"Yeah." His uncle shook his head sadly. "Maybe it's the liquor, but for once I'm going to say what's in my heart. When you became a cop it almost killed me."

Every time he saw his uncle he got the same stupid song. But this time he had to sweat it out.

"Vince, your father was a great lawyer. The best lawyer in Sicily. He could of been the richest, too, only he didn't care for money. He took any case, with or without money, just as long as he was sure the man was innocent. You know what a famous judge in Palermo once said?"

He knew but there was no use trying to stop his uncle.

"This judge said, 'If the lawyer Milazzo takes a case don't bother with the trial. The man is innocent.' That was your father."

His uncle puffed on his big cigar and talked again.

"So your father had trouble with the local Black Hand. They wanted him to work for them but your father said no. They were a tough bunch. They killed your grandfather and burned the farm. Even with his good name your father couldn't buck the Mafia."

His uncle shook his head sadly.

"If he listened to me, your father would of worked with them. He would of become rich. Instead he ran away to America so the Black Hand would leave the rest of the family in peace.

"Your father was some educated man. He spoke Italian, Greek, Spanish and Portuguese, but no English. In Sicily he was respected. Here in America he was just another wop.

"So your father took his little money and opened a coffee shop. When his friends saw him standing behind the counter in a white apron they cried. Such a great man selling coffee. He would say the dignity is in the man, not in the profession. Your father was full of smart sayings, but what did it get him?"

His uncle reached over and dropped the ash from his cigar into one of the empty paper cups.

"Your father tried to go to school here in America, but he had to give it up to make a living. I tried to help him. I got some connections lined up who could get him past his bar examination. But not your father. It had to be the honest way. So he died a poor man. And you, Vince? Will you be the same?"

"I guess so."

"What's it going to get you, being an honest cop? A bullet in the back?"

"What did you have in mind, Uncle Ralph?"

"Get smart. There's lots of cops who go in for what they can get."

"How long do they last?"

"A year." His uncle pulled the big cigar out of his mouth. "But in a year you can stash fifty grand away. That means a house, a wife, a car, a television set. Vince, there's a lot of people in town who would like to do business with you. And when you get shoved off the force, what the hell, a guy like you can always pick up a fast buck. Look at me."

"I am looking at you, Uncle Ralph."

"Then the answer is yes?"

"The answer is no."

His uncle threw his half-finished cigar down on the floor. "Stubborn. Just like your father."

Well, he had listened. Now it was time to go to work.

"Uncle Ralph, you and Tony Statella hung around with the same crowd."

"Me? What kind of a crack is that to make about an uncle?"

"You belonged to the same club."

"Oh, the club." His uncle smiled. "Hell, we got over sixty members."

"What did you think of Tony?"

"Big mouth," his uncle said. "Talked too much and always acted like a big-shot. He got a bad name last month in the club."

"How come?"

"Every year we throw a stag party. You know, drinks and skits and we talk over old times. This year Tony was in charge of entertainment. He started off with a movie picture. This girl is reading a book and the bell rings. She opens the door and it's a girl friend and two sailors. They start making love right in front of the camera. Soon they're undressed."

"I know, Uncle Ralph. I've seen smokies before."

"But not like this." His uncle was all excited. "The bell rang again and a girl comes in with a big dog. What a picture! It went for an hour and a half and I got dizzy trying to keep track of who was doing what."

"So you got a bang out of it."

"Me?" His uncle clapped his hand over his heart. "It made me sick. I like a joke, but most of the guys in the club have grandchildren. It was a shame. And that was only the beginning. Tony had a live show too. Some strippers and then a naked girl made music on a mouth organ. But you'd never guess how."

"I know how, Uncle Ralph."

"You do?" His uncle shrugged. "Well, there were six acts. All beautiful girls. Like movie stars, and young—maybe eighteen. One girl took four apples." His uncle started to laugh. "It kills me every time I think what she done."

"But the club members didn't like it."

"We hated it. Bad taste. Then when the show was over these naked kids came down to the tables and hustled. They'd sit on a guy's lap, horse around, then drag him off to the side rooms. Most of the guys were drunk. The next day when the club finally sobered up they realized they had been suckered good. Those girls took us for about ten grand."

"Some party."

"Tony was buck-crazy. He should of told the girls to take it a little easy. I mean it was his own club. He should of showed some respect."

"What else do you know about Tony's business?"

His uncle looked surprised.

"Was that his business?"

"That and blackmail and a phony singing school and a model agency."

"I didn't know that, Vince."

"You didn't?" He looked his uncle over carefully. "And I suppose you don't know anything about Rocky Tosco?"

"That I know." His uncle smiled. "You should learn from him. Rocky's smart. Knows all the right people."

"Who are the right people? Who keeps that after-hour joint open for him?"

"I don't know, Vince. Maybe he works it through Nice John."

"What's Nice John got to do with it?"

"Nice John is the local don. That's his territory. He's boss of everything crooked that goes on down there."

"Maybe Rocky works direct with the cops? Did you ever hear of a Detective Scotti?"

"Honest, Vince, you know a hell of a lot more than me."

"You'd be surprised if you knew how much I know. And I'll know plenty more before the day is done. I'm out to smash this sex syndicate wide open. But what's wrong with you, Uncle Ralph? All these years I've been trying to stop you talking. Now when I want you to talk you clam up."

His uncle banged his fist on the desk.

"That's no way to speak to an uncle."

"Uncle Ralph, why are you so scared?"

"All right. I'll come right out and tell you. I'm scared for you."

"For me?"

"Why do you think I invited you to my house in Long Island? I wanted to get you off the streets. Why do you think I'm trying to talk you into making a deal? It's because I'm trying to save you. An hour ago, Frank Betti was here for a drink and he broke the news. You've been stepping on toes. Lots of important people don't like you anymore. The word's gone out on you, Vince."

"So they'll bust me off the force."

"Worse than that."

"They're going to beat me up."

"No, Vince. They're out to kill you."

"You're crazy."

"It's the truth. Whoever they are they mean business. But it doesn't have to be that way. You got something on them. Keep your mouth shut and swing a deal. For that I bet they'll give you fifty grand."

"Fifty grand?"

It made him think. Half that money would get Pete Rossi the best lawyer. And with the twenty-five thousand that was left he could marry Gina.

"That's a lot of money."

"Now you're talking, Vince. I went to your father's funeral; I don't want to go to yours. Be smart. Pick up the phone and make a deal with Rocky Tosco."

"And if I don't?"

"The talk going around says you'll be dead by morning."

He got up and smiled. "I'd rather take the bullet."

He opened the door and left the office.

"You're stubborn," his uncle shouted after him. "You're just like your father."

The big-breasted girl in the red smock was waiting for him. She blocked the aisle in front of the water cooler, making like she was getting a drink.

"Excuse me," he said.

"What did you do?"

"Nothing. I want to get by."

She gave him just enough room so he had to brush against her and get a nose full of her toilet water. When he opened the door the bell rang and over the sound he heard the girl.

"He must be married," the girl said. "Did you see the sour look on his puss?"

He walked down the stairs slowly trying to figure it out. No one was so quick to finger a cop these days. In the last few hours he had kicked a raw nerve and frightened people. Frightened them bad enough to make them want to kill him.

But who the hell were they?

Outside the snow had stopped falling, but the wind was as cold as death. When he got into the car he slammed the door so hard the glove compartment dropped open. He kicked it shut with his knee and then looked at the clock on the dashboard.

Ten to five. He had thirteen hours to go. Maybe less.

The word was out that he'd be dead by tomorrow morning. An icepick in the back, or a bullet singing through the air, or a car smashing him down.

He took his handkerchief out and wiped his face and around his collar.

He shoved the handkerchief into his pocket quickly. He was angry at himself for letting someone get an idea of what was going on inside.

"Where to now?" Whiteman asked.

"You go back to the station house and check out."

"And you?"

"I'm going uptown to see Nice John."

"I'll take you."

"Look, Whiteman, I might be on this all night."

"That's what I figured. So I went across the street and phoned the wife. Told her I'd try to be home for Christmas breakfast."

He looked at Whiteman's ugly face and got a funny feeling. It was good to know he wasn't alone in the world after all. He wanted to thank the guy, but he couldn't. It had been so long since he tried he had forgotten how to say anything nice.

"Then, what the hell are we waiting for?" he finally asked.

"Okay," Whiteman said. "Uptown and Nice John."

"I'm freezing," Whiteman said. "And you're sweating."

The doorman in front of the fancy apartment house was big enough to handle a football team.

The elevator man was big too.

"Going up, sir?" He pointed to his elevator.

"I'm using the private one in the back."

"Yes, sir." The guy was polite but he snapped his fingers real loud.

Out of the dark shadows came another big man.

"Help you, chum?" he asked.

"I want to see Nice John."

The guy was looking him over, frisking him with his eyes. Then he turned to a phone on the wall.

"What's your name and business, chum?"

"My name is Milazzo. My business is my own."

"Hello, Peanuts." The guy said into the phone. "There's a Milazzo down here. Wants to see the boss. He looks like a bull."

When the guy hung up he pointed to the private elevator.

He walked in and pushed the button marked Penthouse. While the car went up he slipped off his coat and pulled the gun out of its holster. It saved time. Besides he didn't like punks pawing him.

When the elevator opened he stepped out into the hall and two men were waiting. He handed the coat and gun over. "Is that all you carry?" one of them asked.

"That's all."

"Mind if I touch you up a bit?"

"I'd rather you didn't."

"If Milazzo says he's unloaded, he's unloaded." It was Nice John standing in the open door smiling and holding out both his hands. "Come on in, Vincent."

They shook hands, and Nice John put his arm around his back and walked him into the place.

The room was big enough for a basketball game. The windows started at the floor and reached the ceiling. Through them he could see out over the city. Lots of lights were going on. It was getting late.

"Since you been here," Nice John said, "I did the place over. You like it?"

He looked around. The furniture was low, simple, modern stuff. Everything was quiet and neat.

"Good taste, Nice John," he said.

Nice John smiled.

"It's the new style. Everything looks plain, but it costs plenty. Sit down, Vincent."

He sat down on the big circular couch that faced the white brick fireplace.

"The fire smells good."

"That I didn't pay for. God put the sweet smell in the wood."

Nice John started to pace the big room. He was surprised at how old the guy looked.

To the world Nice John was a public enemy, but back

in the old days he and all the other kids in Little Italy looked up to Nice John as if he were Robin Hood. They knew he stole and killed. They knew he controlled every crime along the Atlantic coast down to Florida. But they also knew their fathers went to Nice John when they were in real trouble. He was the guy who sent one kid through college and paid for another kid's operation. Nice John was their hero.

Whenever his big black car went through the streets kids came running to be there when the door opened. And Nice John never disappointed them. He knew most of them by name. Those he didn't know he asked and he usually knew their fathers.

"Vincent," Nice John once said real loud so the whole street could hear. "Milazzo is a good name. Your father was a great man."

But that was in the old days when Nice John was riding high. In the last few years there had been lots of trouble. And even though Nice John had been too tricky to get caught, he was on the way down.

And he looked it. His shoulders were sagging, and so was the skin on his face. What was left of his hair was white. The guy was going fast and he twitched and jerked like a first offender waiting sentence.

"Why don't you get out of the rackets, Nice John?"

"Two years ago I got the urge," Nice John said. "I was making a trip to Florida and my car blew a tire. While the boys worked it over I got out to stretch my legs. It was in a dead town, but it had wide streets, big lawns and palm trees." Nice John waved his hand. "I made up my mind. I turned the car around and went back to New York."

Nice John had reached the end of the big room. He stopped talking and stared at the wall. Then slowly he turned and started walking back again.

"In New York I split my business with my four top

boys. I said the first one who takes a bad step, I myself, Nice John, in person, will put the bullet in their head. Then I hurried back to the little town in Florida. I picked a nice lot and a good builder. I didn't want much. Just a little house and a big lawn. You know why I wanted the big lawn, Vincent?"

"No, I don't."

"Because I wanted to plant things and watch them grow. I think the nicest thing is to watch a little flower be born. Crazy, huh? Me, Nice John, talking like this. But that's what I wanted. To be alone and in peace."

He reached the big windows that looked out over the city and stood there silently for a long time.

"The dream didn't last, Vincent," he finally said bitterly. "Some stinking reporter on some stinking local paper heard whose house it was. I explained real nice to the jerk I didn't want any publicity. I just wanted to be left alone. So what's this reporter do? He blasts the story in his stinking sheet. The mothers' clubs and the teachers get together and sign petitions. Everybody in the stinking little town gangs up to stop me from building."

He turned away from the window.

"Me, Nice John!" He hit his chest with his fist. "Run out of a town by women and a long-hair reporter who isn't smart enough to wipe his glasses. What the hell. I couldn't retire anyway. When I got back to New York it was a mess. The four punks were ready to dig trenches in the street and start a war. It's all forgotten. How about a drink, Vincent? What do you want?"

"Whatever you have."

"Me?" Nice John laughed sadly. "I drink milk. I got a feeling like there's a hundred feet of heavy rope in my stomach and someone is pulling it out through my mouth."

"I know what you mean, Nice John." He was staring at

the fancy watch on the desk. Twenty minutes after five. Another half-hour shot. "I'll have milk too."

Nice John walked to the desk and flipped a switch on a box.

"Peanuts, bring in a bottle of milk and three glasses. But first take the chill off the milk."

Nice John walked back and stood in front of the fireplace.

"It sits better on the stomach without the chill. Me, once I could wash down hot peppers with a glass of Scotch. Now cold milk gives me a cramp."

He started walking again.

"Did I ever tell you how I got the name Nice John?"

"No."

"When I was starting there were two other Johns in the gang. Big John, Little John, and me. It was in the days they first came out with those nickel slots on the toilets. If a guy was cheap he used the free toilet. So for a joke they called me Free John. I hated it, but they were bigger."

He stopped and stood there looking at the wall in front of him.

"Then some hijackers tied Big John in one of his trucks and set fire to it. That left Little John and me. We had a talk, and Little John died. I became number one of the gang. That's when I changed my name. I wanted something friendly, so I picked Nice."

He turned away from the wall and smiled.

"When people call me Nice John, even if they hate my guts, it makes me feel liked."

This time he changed his direction and started pacing the width of the room.

"From a wop greenhorn who dug ditches fourteen hours a day so the foreman could steal half my pay I smashed my way up to kingpin. Me!" He hit his chest. "Judges, mayors, governors, they all licked my shoes. Yes, Nice

John. Whatever you say, Nice John. If I just raised my voice they got so scared they had to change their underwear."

He reached the wall again.

"I had five thousand names on my payroll. Elevator boys, janitors, ordinary working guys all over picking up a few buck bringing numbers to my runners. Candy stores, drug stores, cigar stores, all the owners got their cuts when my bookies hung out in their joints. The cops on the beat, the cops at the desk, the ward heelers and the politicians in City Hall, the lawyers, the judges. Everybody wanted to be a partner with Nice John."

He turned away from the wall, shaking his head.

"So what happens? Some citizens' group and a couple of newspapers start raising a stink. I get an invite to go to Washington and testify on my business. My high-price lawyer tells me I got to go because of public opinion."

He threw his hands in the air and then let them fall.

"Now when I ask a judge or a politician for a little favor I get a ride. Sorry, Nice John, we can't. It will make a stink if the people find out. What will we tell the new investigating committee? So all because of public opinion my connections are gone. My protection is shot. My business is ruined. Whoever thought the people could be so strong?"

"And now that I'm on my way down everybody comes running to put more wax on my skids. Guys I took off the street, guys who I put where they are—they're the worst. They want to see me get it so they'll feel safe. Then they can act like honest men. They're all out to get me."

There was a knock on the door.

Nice John went to the box on the desk and touched a button. A bright light went on over the door and suddenly he realized the door was glass because he could see a man standing on the other side holding a tray.

Nice John touched another button. The light went out and the door swung open.

"Put the milk on the table, Peanuts."

The man put the tray down and started to go.

"Stick around, Peanuts." Nice John looked at the bottle of milk and smiled. "Yeah. I got lots of people who'd like to see me dead. Where is it coming from? A rifle slug through the window?" Nice John shook his head. "The glass is bulletproof. Is it going to be a bomb in my car?" Nice John shook his head again. "No. I own a rental agency. I have over sixty cars to pick from. They can't guess which car I'll use. Maybe someone will fly over in one of those helicopters and try to drop a bomb? It will be tough on them. I got a couple of fifty-caliber machine guns up there. Or maybe it's in the milk. Maybe that's how they're trying to do it this time."

Nice John pointed to the milk.

"Go ahead, Peanuts, taste it."

Slowly and with shaking hand the man poured some milk.

Then even more slowly he brought the glass to his lips.

"Go ahead—swallow," Nice John said. "There's a stomach pump in the toilet."

With a quick jerk of his head the man swallowed some of the milk.

"Okay," Nice John said. "Go sit in the corner."

The man went to a chair and sat down.

"My old aunt is the only one allowed in the kitchen," Nice John said. "She's almost seventy-five. Blind as a coffin, deaf as a gravestone, and she's a lousy cook. But who eats, anyway? I live on milk. For exercise I walk."

Nice John looked around.

"I got fourteen rooms here. I know the measurements of each room. I should. I walk them enough. You know what I say? I got the fanciest prison any jailbird ever had."

He started walking.

"A jail, Vincent, that's what it is. How do you feel, Peanuts?"

"I feel good, boss."

"Take is easy, You may die in a few minutes."

"Yes, boss."

Nice John came over and sat down on the big circular couch.

"Here it is Christmas Eve and I got no one to talk to but you, Vincent, because we got something in common. You're an honest cop and I'm an honest crook."

"I have another reason for liking you, Nice John."

"Tell me. Maybe it will cheer me up."

"After my father died it was rough going for my mother and me. But we made it because twice when they were going to turn off the gas someone paid the bill, and every week a man came to the house with a basket of groceries. One day I followed the man with the basket and he went to your office."

"So you knew?"

"Why did you do it?"

"I owed it to your father. Once in the old country he did me a favor. A rich neighbor was trying to take my father's farm away. The land had been in our family since Sicily came out of the water. But the neighbor was rich and the local judge was crooked.

"'Give me money,' I said to my father. 'I will buy a gun and kill them both.'"

Nice John laughed.

"Even then I was wild. But my father had another idea. We should go to the lawyer Milazzo.

"'A lawyer,' I said. 'Where will we get the money?'

"'The lawyer Milazzo,' my father answered. 'Is a good man.'

"So we went. I was surprised how young your father

was because he already had such a big name. The office was full of crying women, poor farmers, fishermen and miners. We waited for hours but finally we got in.

"Your father was polite. He talked to us like my father was a rich man. He listened to the story and studied the papers.

"'You have nothing to worry about,' he told my father. 'I will take care of it.'

"'Tell him we have no money,' I whispered.

"But your father heard and he smiled and said we could pay when we had it.

"'There are thirteen kids,' I said. 'And three parts of the land is rock. It will take a hundred years to pay.'

"'That is a long time,' your father said. 'But since you are thinking about the money I can forget it. There is no need for both of us to worry.'

"When we got outside, my father hit me across the back of the head.

"'That's to teach you to be so smart,' he said. 'Now maybe you'll believe there are good people left in the world.'

"Well, your father saved our farm but I got into trouble of my own and I ran away to America. I did good too. But I never forgot the lawyer Milazzo. You can imagine how bad I felt one day when I walked into a coffee shop and saw him in a white apron serving demitasse.

"He wouldn't let me give him anything. Then I got an idea. I went to your Uncle Ralph." Nice John stopped a moment, then shrugged. "Vincent, I hate to say this about your uncle, but the guy stinks."

"I know what you mean."

"I had Ralph tell your father that he could fix the bar examination, but your father wouldn't do something crooked. So that's the way it was until I heard the crazy news they had thrown your father in jail."

Nice John jumped up from the couch.

"Can you imagine my surprise? The lawyer Milazzo arrested. And what a stinking rap. They found a bottle of homemade anisette behind the counter of the coffee shop. The whole country's bathing in the river because every bathtub is full of bootleg hootch and they arrest the lawyer Milazzo because he used a little anisette in his coffee to kill his cough.

"I knew right away it was a frame. I sent my lawyer to help but your father wouldn't talk. They sent him away for nine months. When he got out his cough was worse. A year later he died, but he never said who put the frame on him."

"I knew who framed my father."

"How did you know?"

"I figured it out. One day Rocky Tosco's father came in. You remember him? The big fat butcher? He wanted my father to sell bootleg whiskey from the back room. My father wouldn't listen so old man Tosco tried to get rough. My father was a quiet man but he was strong. He grabbed Tosco by the neck and threw him out into the street. Three days later the prohibition agents came and made the pinch."

He took the pipe from his pocket and slowly filled it.

"I was only a kid but I told my father I was going to kill the butcher.

"'Killing a man,' my father told me, 'never solved anything. It will only make you as bad as Tosco. Vincent, you must never lose your self-respect. Never sell it or throw it away. When you have it you are as good as any man and you can always look up into the face of God.'"

He put his pipe in his mouth and lit it.

"Two days after my father was sentenced Rocky Tosco stood in the door of the butcher shop and screamed, 'How's your jailbird father?' When I ran after him he ducked inside the store.

"I waited for him after school but he spotted me and told the principal. They made me wait in my class half an hour each day to give Rocky time to get home."

He took the pipe out of his mouth. It was as bitter-tasting as his memories. He knocked the tobacco out and put the pipe away.

"One day I saw Rocky in a lot. I chased him until I caught him. As big as he was I started to pound the hell out of him. But one of his friends ran to the butcher shop and told Rocky's older brother. The big potato came running and grabbed me and held me so Rocky could tear me apart. Beating me silly wasn't enough. While I was lying in the dirt Rocky kicked me in the head."

He ran his fingers over the scar.

"Self-respect, Nice John. It's the hardest thing in the world to keep. Rocky Tosco still goes around laughing in my face. And his old man killed my father."

"Cheer up, Vincent," Nice John said. "I got a Christmas present for you. Something to make you feel good. Old man Tosco died because he ratted on your father."

Nice John laughed and started walking again.

"I didn't know about Tosco and your father until a few years later. One of my truck drivers told me he used to be a prohibition agent. We got to talking about old times and he said he was one of the guys that raided your father's place. He also told me that old man Tosco was the guy that phoned in the tip.

"That made me think. Suddenly I remembered that the night the Brown brothers and me sat in a speakeasy closing a deal for the alcohol in my Long Island warehouse, Tosco, the slob, was sitting at the next table. And three hours later the Feds raided the warehouse and my kid brother was killed. It all added up. Old man Tosco was a stool pigeon.

"That's all I needed. I grabbed four of my boys and we went to Tosco's butcher shop. He was so scared we had to untie his apron and put his coat on for him. Then we took him to Long Island. The same warehouse where my kid brother died. The boys took off Tosco's shoes and put each foot in a pail. And he stood there watching while they mixed the cement."

Nice John stopped walking.

"Vincent, did you ever see a piece of suet that's been laying in the sun? It gets a wet layer of grease over it. That was Tosco. It took maybe an hour for the cement to dry in the pails. He prayed. He begged. He cried. And I just watched.

"Then the boys carried him out to the beach and into the water up to his waist. It was one o'clock in the morning and the tide was coming in. I stood there listening to his screams. In about an hour he stopped screaming. He made a couple of bubbles. Then it was over. I had paid up two debts. The cement on the right foot was for my brother. The cement on the left foot was for the lawyer Milazzo. I thought you might like to know about it."

"Thanks, Nice John."

"Forget it. And now, Vincent, tell me what did you come for?"

"I just found out the word is out to kill me."

"You? A cop? They must be desperate."

"You don't know about it?"

"No. And that's the truth."

"Nice John, was Tony Statella one of your boys?"

"That stinking pot. He couldn't handle my toilet paper concession. The guy was no good. Him and his combination. You remember what I said about the filthy fifties? Those are the apes I'm talking about. Nothing is too dirty for them. I hear they contacted all the abortionists in the country. Told them they'd give a hundred bucks for each girl steered their way. The filthy fifties. I get sick at the way they work."

"Who's the Number One of the combination?"

"That I don't know."

"What about Rocky Tosco?"

"He stinks too."

"Do you give him the protection for his restaurant?"

"I wouldn't kick him with your shoe."

"Then who is his connection?"

"That's a funny question. One story says he's got a cop named Scotti working for him. The other story says Scotti can't be bought. Give me a call tomorrow and I'll see if I can dig up any more dirt."

He looked at the fancy clock on the desk.

"Thanks, Nice John, but tomorrow will be too late. And I've got to go now."

"Wait," Nice John said. "We forgot our drink. Hey, Peanuts, how do you feel?"

"Real good, boss."

"Come here."

The man came over and Nice John looked into his eyes. Then he made the man hold out his hand.

"He doesn't look worse than usual. How about it, Vincent, a drink of milk for old times?"

"Sure."

Nice John poured.

"Merry Christmas, Nice John."

"Merry Christmas, Vincent."

They both drank. Then Nice John looked at his empty glass. "And if it was poisoned," Nice John smiled, "may God have mercy on my soul."

Down in the street he found the car empty. Whiteman was gone.

He started toward the corner to see if his partner was

there, but he stopped. The street looked so long and dark. A man with his coat collar turned up was standing near a service entrance. Down the other way a couple of fellows stood talking alongside a delivery truck.

Instead of walking he got inside the car.

The clock on the dashboard said seven-twenty.

He had been with Nice John over two hours. He had learned a lot, but nothing important. Or was it important? He was so mixed up he didn't know anymore.

Then suddenly he heard footsteps. Someone was coming down the street. He swung around quickly, and saw it was three young kids. They walked by talking and laughing. They were laughing so much they must be up to something. They'd probably be on the police line-up tomorrow morning.

Where the hell was Whiteman?

Time was getting short and there was so much to do. Somewhere during the day he had come close. So close they were out to kill him.

He started with Tony Statella's body and tried to remember everything that had happened. There was Rocky, and the hat check girl, the stoolies, Scotti, the thief, and Bell from the district attorney's office. And by the time he reached his uncle the word was out to get him. But who was it?

Suddenly he thought of someone he left off the list. Whiteman.

All that talk his partner gave him about letting Rocky alone, telling him to lay off the syndicate, and then calling his wife up so he could stay the rest of the night.

Was Whiteman out there now calling someone, getting him set up like a tin can on a fence for target practice?

That was the hell of it. You never knew who your friends were or who was out to do you. The best thing was to play it safe all the way and trust no one.

He was wiping his face with his handkerchief when he saw Whiteman's heavy figure coming down the street. He shoved the handkerchief in his pocket and waited.

"I was cold," Whiteman said as he got into the car. "So I went to the corner for a cup of coffee. I figured you'd come looking for me."

"I just got here myself."

"Where to, Vince?"

That question again. If this was a book he would get all the suspects together in a room and sweat it out of them. But this wasn't a book. And he couldn't go back to the beginning and start over again because there wasn't time.

"Vince, how about going around to the neighborhood. It's dark now. Maybe some pigeon will find the guts to contact you."

"Okay," he said.

It sounded like a good idea. Or was it a trap?

Whiteman parked in front of the dark vegetable store and they waited.

The street lights were on. Christmas trees were shining in the windows. People were loaded down with packages and hurrying home. On the corner a couple of grimy panhandlers were begging.

"Those bums," he said. "Every year there's more of them and they get braver and come further away from the Bowery."

"What the hell?" Whiteman said. "It's Christmas for them too."

He looked at the clock on the dashboard. The hands were moving, but nothing else happened.

"Maybe," Whiteman said. "If you get out and walk around someone will contact you."

Contact him, or kill him.

"I'll stay right here," he said.

"It's okay with me."

They sat in silence. Then suddenly Whiteman pointed. "Look, Vincent."

He looked and saw the familiar figure.

"That's Paul Tosco," Whiteman said. "Rocky's kid brother. Maybe he can give you a line."

"Let's go."

When the car was alongside of Rocky's kid brother he rolled down the window.

"Paul."

The guy stopped and swung around. Even the darkness and the thick glasses couldn't hide the fear in his eyes.

"Yes, Detective."

"Keep walking up the street until I stop you."

The guy started walking.

"Stay behind him, Whiteman. I want to see if he's being followed."

He made Paul Tosco walk three windswept blocks before he felt sure it wasn't a trap.

"All right, Whiteman, stop here."

The car pulled to the curb and he jumped out and motioned Paul into the car. The guy slipped in next to Whiteman. Then he followed.

Stumbling on Paul Tosco like this was very pat. It had a bit of a smell. He wasn't going to take any chances sitting in the middle. It was better near a door. If something happened he had a chance to drop out and shoot back.

"What's up, Detective?"

"I want to talk to you about your brother."

"I don't know anything, Detective. Rocky and I don't get along."

"Has he beat you up lately?"

"He don't touch me." Paul looked down at his hands. "No more, he don't."

"Why not?"

"Because I stay away from him."

"Tell me about your brother's business."

"I don't know a thing. Rocky don't trust me."

"Is it because you ratted on the LaSalle brothers?"

Paul took a quick look at Whiteman, then turned around and looked at him. His weak eyes were full of panic.

"Gee, Detective, that's no way to talk."

"Should I get out of the car?" Whiteman asked.

"You stay right there," he said. "I like things the way they are. Nice and comfortable. So Rocky figured out you squealed on them."

"You got your pinch, Detective. I was only doing my duty."

"You did it because they shortchanged you on your cut. And I put them away for three years. One of the brothers lives right around the block. I wonder what he'd do if I told him."

"Detective, you promised."

"I keep my promises."

"I know you do." Paul sighed and relaxed.

"But my partner here didn't promise, and now he knows."

"That's a dirty trick."

"Tell me about your brother's business."

"All I know is Rocky decided to go into the restaurant racket three years ago."

"Where did he get the dough?"

"Working with the LaSalle brothers. They used to go upstate and knock off a job on the weekends. Sometimes on a big deal they made me drive. Rocky was supposed to be on the job you pinched the LaSalle brothers for, but he got food poisoning and couldn't make it. They took me instead. I had to go. They made me. On the way home they slipped me fifty bucks. They said that was my share. I bitched and they pushed me around. That's why I told you. But I never went out on a job again. I gave it all up and went to work in the post office."

"And Rocky?"

"When you got the brothers he was worried. He figured I told and he almost killed me. Then he decided to stick his money into that cellar restaurant. The guy was going broke, and Rocky picked it up for dirt. But before he took it Rocky went to Detective Scotti and swung a deal."

"What kind of a deal?"

"I don't know. Except he's the guy who covers for Rocky."

"You hear that, Whiteman?"

"I hear, Vince."

"Go on, Paul."

"Well, Rocky started off as an after-hour joint. Good food and drinks. That's when Tony Statella moved in."

"Now it's getting interesting. Go on."

"Tony took on the hat-check concession. He put a cigarette girl and camera girl in. Then all the chorus girls coming down when their shows were over brought a lot of rich society guys. So Tony moved in some of his professional hustlers to take them over."

"Go on."

"Well, that's it. Rocky is stuffing his mattress with dough and I'm working in the post office. He could have made an opening for me, but he won't even let me walk into the joint."

"Who's the Number One of the syndicate?"

"Syndicate?" The guy was really surprised. "All I know about is Tony. Honest."

He opened the door and got out.

"Beat it."

Rocky's brother slipped out fast and hurried away. Then he got back into the car and stared at the clock on the dashboard.

What was it Nice John said? I feel like I got a hundred

feet of rope in my stomach and someone is pulling it out through my mouth. That was just the way he felt.

Suddenly Whiteman moved. He was getting out of the car. He reached over and grabbed the guy's hairy wrist.

"Where you going, Whiteman?"

"What's the matter, Vincent? Do I need permission to go to the toilet?"

Whiteman got out and slammed the door. He watched the heavy figure move across the street and go into a bar. Now he was all alone. He opened his coat and loosened the jacket around his gun.

The clock was moving and he was standing still. Why didn't he do something? Making the deal with Bell was crazy. How could he hope to crack something so big in so short a time? Why didn't he forget about it and just concentrate on his heavy hate—Rocky Tosco.

Maybe he ought to get the gun Pete Rossi used to kill Tony Statella. He could trick Rocky into putting his fingerprints on it. Then with a few crooked witnesses he could frame the guy.

He would watch Rocky sweat through the trial. Then he'd make a trip up to the Big House and sit there watching as they strapped Rocky's legs to the hot seat. They'd put the tin pot on Rocky's head. The lights would dim. The room would fill with a buzzing sound and Rocky's body would do a crazy dance. Then all too soon it would be over.

What was the use of dreaming? He didn't have the money to fix a frame. And what was more important he didn't have the time.

Right now Whiteman might be placing a call to make the final arrangements. Or someone might be waiting in a doorway, or with a rifle on a roof. Or death might be in one of the cars parked along the street.

Where is it coming from, Vincent?

Now he really knew how Nice John felt.

He pulled his handkerchief out and started mopping the sweat....

"Detective."

He spun around in his seat, grabbing at his gun. But it was a cop standing there.

He lowered the window.

"Detective," the cop said. "I'm in trouble. Do you speak Italian?"

"Yeah."

"Well, this little old lady is bending my ear and I can't get what it's all about. Would you speak to her?"

He looked behind the cop and saw the old lady. Her wrinkled face made her look as if she'd been dead ten years. She was wearing a neat black velvet coat with a brown fur collar. There were black knitted gloves on her hands and she cared a portable radio.

He got out of the car and looked down at her.

"You speak Italian?" she asked.

"That's right."

The little old lady leaned back as though she was looking up the side of a skyscraper.

"You a policeman?"

"Yes, ma'am."

"Good. I must make a complaint. I live on this street for many years. Eleven children I have had here. Three did not live. My other eight are all married. I am blessed with twenty-seven grandchildren."

Down the block he could see the big jeweler's clock. It was lit up, but it was too far away to see the hands. That only made him feel the time was moving faster.

"As they married," the old lady went on, "my children left the neighborhood. I now live alone. But it was Christmas and my oldest son said I must visit him. He lives in Newark and he is a good boy. But the girl he married, her people came from Bari. Where are your people from, Officer?"

"From Sicily."

"I knew you were good the moment I saw you. My daughter-in-law cooks everything out of a can. Mamma, my son tells me, you got to stay out of the kitchen. Even for Christmas they wouldn't let me cook. So when no one looked I left the house of my daughter-in-law to come back to spend this day in my own kitchen with my own pots and my memories."

The old lady talked on and he stared at the big clock. The cold was going right through him. Yet he was still sweating. And the old lady was probably so close to death she couldn't feel the cold because she went right on talking.

"At the station where I must change they tell me that four hours will pass before there is another bus to New York City. Four hours to wait, and the battery of my little radio was finished. What was I to do for so long a time?"

He wished the old lady would get to the point.

"Then I remembered the movie near the bus station where they play Italian pictures."

"Italian pictures? In Newark?"

"Sure. I remembered many years ago my son took me there. And I like good Italian pictures. American pictures talk too fast. But Italian pictures I understand. Much singing. Much love. So I went to the movies and I bought a ticket. It used to be thirty cents, but now it costs eighty."

Whiteman came out of the bar and got into the car.

"I went into the movie and sat down. The lights were on and all over were men. Everyone is a man. I think it's Christmas so the women are home cooking. I say to the man next to me to put away his cigar. And to the men in front of me I tell not to make so much smoke."

"Look, mother," he said. "I am very busy."

"Sure, Officer. I come to the story. I wait for the picture but a man is selling candy. He talked more than I talk. I thought to buy a box of his candy but then he tells how with each box he gives pictures and books and maybe even a dollar. I put my money away. If candy needs so much to make you buy, the candy is no good."

By morning he was supposed to be dead.

Why didn't he go and have it out with Rocky face to face? If he had to die, at least he could take the rat with him.

He looked down the street. It was two blocks to Rocky's cellar. Then he smiled at the old lady.

Hot as the killers were, it was a good chance they wouldn't shoot at him while she was around.

"It's cold standing here," he said. "Could you walk and talk?"

"I can always talk."

He took her arm and turned her toward Rocky's place, and together they started down the street.

"So then what happened?" he asked.

"Finally the man with candy went away, and music starts. Now I think I'll see a good Italian picture. Instead girls come out. Mother of mine! Bathing clothes are bad, but the bodies of these girls had on even less. I wouldn't walk by my husband in such things and we had eleven children together."

He stopped her at the curb and looked around. The cold street was pretty quiet. A couple of men were on a stoop talking. A kid was running home with a can of olive oil.

Then suddenly one of the men pointed at him.

For a second he was ready to hit the ground but the man waved. He looked again and waved back. He knew the guy. They had gone to school together.

He helped the old lady across the street and she kept

talking.

"Then a girl comes out and she sings. She sings terrible like something hurts in her stomach. All of a sudden, you must believe me, Officer, this girl's dress begins to fall apart. I want to jump up and tell her but she catches a piece of dress in time and holds it in front of her. So you think she would run in shame. But no. Even with her terrible voice and ripped dress she must stay and finish her song. And the men scream like animals."

The old lady shook her head in disgust and went on.

"I jumped up and told them to be quiet. I told them they should be ashamed. They shut up I tell you."

Suddenly in a store window he saw the reflection of headlights. A car was following them. He turned quickly, keeping the old lady in front of him.

It was Whiteman in the police car. His partner pulled to the curb.

"What do you want, Whiteman?" He had his hand inside his coat.

"I followed so you wouldn't have to walk back in the cold."

"Park where you are. I'm talking to the lady."

Whiteman smiled.

"She's a little old for a pigeon, Vince."

"I like her company. You wait here. I'll be back."

He took the old lady's arm and started walking again.

"Well, Officer, this girl did things." She stopped talking and looked at him. "Officer, are you married?"

"No."

"Better I don't tell you what she did."

They passed under the jeweler's big watch and now he could see the hands clearly.

Eight-thirty.

Sometime between then and morning he was supposed to be dead—and across the street was Rocky's place.

"More girls came out," the old lady said. "And they did bad dances. Believe me, Officer, a baby in a diaper is more covered. Two hours I sat watching. It made me sick."

The old lady was getting on his nerves.

"What in hell did you stay for?" he asked.

"I was waiting for the Italian picture."

He took her arm and walked her across the street. Together they stood there and he looked down the stairs that led to the cellar.

Now there was nothing left to do but get rid of his shield and find Rocky.

"So what do you want?" he asked the old lady.

"I want my eighty cents back."

He reached for his wallet and held out a dollar.

"I want my own money," she said.

"Take this. Tomorrow I'll go to the place and they will give it back to me."

"Oh." The old lady took the dollar but she didn't leave. Instead she poked around in her black leather bag and found two dimes. "I do not want charity. Here is your change."

He sighed and took the two dimes.

"What's your name, Officer?"

"Milazzo."

He kept looking down the stairs.

"That's a good name. There was once a great lawyer by that name."

"He was my father."

Why the hell didn't she go?

"You're a very good boy." The old lady leaned over and patted his hand. "Your father would be proud of you."

He watched her going down the street until she finally disappeared around the corner.

Your father would be proud of you.

The words kept bouncing in his head.

He turned away from the stairs that led to Rocky and he started walking.

He walked and walked until he came to a small park. He sat down on a bench and closed his eyes real tight.

Never lose your self-respect. Never sell it or throw it away. When you have it you are as good as any man and you can always look up into the face of God.

All day he had been looking for a miracle. Testing God.

And why? Was he trying to bust a filthy crime syndicate to be a good cop? No! It was just to get revenge on Rocky Tosco. For that he was willing to throw his life away, his job, his self-respect.

Slowly the cold air cooled his face. The fire in his stomach simmered down.

For the first time that day he heard the sound of the church bells that had been heralding Christmas. He opened his eyes. The snow in the little park where no one had walked was pure and white.

What he had to do was simple. He had to go back and arrest Pete Rossi for murder. That was his job.

The rest was up to society. He'd have to make Gina realize that. It wouldn't be easy, but whoever said a cop's life was an easy one.

His father had words for that too.

The dignity is in the man, not in the profession.

In the meantime let Rocky laugh. Detective Scotti couldn't protect him forever. And why was a nice guy like Scotti working for a rat like Rocky?

Then suddenly he smiled, because he had the answer.

He had been looking for a miracle to satisfy his heavy hate, and now that he admitted he was wrong the miracle came to him.

A simple thought, as clear and sweet as the sound of the

church bells rolling over the city.

He understood what the chief was trying to tell him with that story about the undercover agent. He should have caught on right away because he had swung the same deal with Al Walsh the gambler. Lots of cops did it—why not a smart cop like Scotti?

Rocky's joint was never touched. Rocky was being protected by the police because he worked for them.

Rocky Tosco was Scotti's stool pigeon.

PART FOUR

On the way back to the car he stopped at a drug store and called headquarters. In a few minutes they gave him Scotti's address.

Scotti lived way out in Astoria. It would take an hour to get there and another to get back.

Time was so short. He left the drug store wondering if he could make it, and suddenly he got a funny feeling, like a wet hand on the back of his neck. Something was wrong.

Then he saw that down the block a figure had broken away from the shadow of a doorway.

He walked a little more and the figure moved forward. It was a man waiting for him to pass.

Quickly he turned and headed back to the drug store. At the corner he stopped to check. The man was no longer hiding. He was out in the open, coming right after him. To be so brave the guy must be coked to the gills. Who else but a dope fiend could they get to kill a cop?

He turned the corner and started around the block to get to the car. As he hurried he looked back once more. The guy was still there, still following.

When he finally reached the car he yanked the door

open so hard the hinges complained. He jumped in and even before the door was dosed he hollered.

"Let's go."

"What's up, Vince?"

"Cut the gab and hit the gas."

As they took off he swung around to look out the back window. The street was quiet, except for a taxi that was pulling away from the curb.

"What's it all about, Vince?"

As he caught his breath he looked Whiteman over. Then he decided he had nothing to lose so he told him.

"They're out to kill me."

"You? A cop! You're crazy!"

"If I'm so crazy check and see if we're being tailed."

Whiteman looked in the mirror. Then he turned into an alley. When they came out the other side the cab was still behind them.

"You're right, Vince."

"Well then, shake them."

"Shake them? Are you nuts? Let's go back and see what they want."

He put his hand inside his jacket and felt his gun.

"I know what they want, Whiteman, and I say shake them."

Whiteman's jaw went hard and his hand went tight on the wheel. He kicked off the siren and rubbed hell out of the taxpayers' tires taking sharp turns.

"Okay," Whiteman said after a while. "I lost them."

"Good. Now we go out to Astoria."

"You know, Vince," Whiteman said slowly, "I feel sick. I hate running away from a fight."

He knew how the guy felt. But there wasn't enough time left to start swapping slugs with a hophead.

Scotti lived in a new housing development.

Everyone had fixed their lawns differently and the houses were painted in different colors. But as much as they tried to hide it, the small houses all looked alike.

He used the spotlight a couple of times to pick out numbers until they found Scotti's place. As he went up the walk he noticed the lights were out except the Christmas tree in the window. He rang the bell, hoping the guy was home.

The second time he rang he heard someone coming downstairs and then a voice asked who it was.

"Detective Milazzo."

The door opened and Scotti stood there in his bare feet and bathrobe. With his eyes full of sleep and his hair mussed the guy looked like a kid.

"I didn't think you'd be sleeping so early."

"You know how it is. A cop sleeps when he can." Scotti opened the door wide. "Come on in."

He walked into the little hall and started to take off his oat.

"First, Scotti, I'm sorry I woke you. And second I'm sorry for the way I talked to you this afternoon."

"Forget it."

Scotti hung his coat in the closet and put his hat on the telephone table. They were going into the living room when a soft voice called from the top of the stairs.

"Ted. You forgot your slippers."

Scotti looked down at his bare feet and smiled.

"That's the boss. I better go up and get them."

When Scotti left he walked into the living room and looked around. It was small and only half furnished. He smiled sadly. On a cop's salary it would be wedding presents and time payments.

It wasn't fancy. But the candy dish was full. There were cigarettes in the cigarette box. He tried the lighter and it worked on the first click. The floor was polished like glass. The Christmas tree was trimmed in silver and blue. And on the side table he found a white album. He flipped the cover over and there was a picture of Scotti and his wife standing in front of the altar being married.

So this was the way some cops lived.

When Scotti came in they sat down and he didn't waste any time.

"I'll give it to you straight, Scotti. I know Rocky Tosco is stooling for you."

Scotti's hands pulled the belt tighter on the bathrobe but not a muscle moved in his face.

"Milazzo, I don't know what you're saying."

"The chief as much as told me, Scotti."

The guy changed. The smile went and a film of ice dropped over his eyes. He didn't look so good-natured anymore. In fact he looked plenty mean.

"What did the chief tell you, Milazzo?"

"Don't get me wrong, Scotti. The chief didn't spill any soup. He just told me to lay off you and Rocky or I'd be busted by six o'clock this morning."

"The chief is a smart man. Why didn't you listen?"

"Look, Scotti. I'm willing to forget your little setup. But first you've got to give me some information. I don't know why you and the chief are holding it back. Maybe you're waiting for election, so you can break it with a lot of headlines. But I can't wait. I need that information right now."

"What information are you talking about?"

"I want the stuff on the sex syndicate."

"Sex syndicate? You're on the wrong subway, Milazzo."

"Don't play coy, Scotti. I know Rocky is up to his greasy hair in the combination."

"What combination?"

"You mean you don't know about Tony Statella? About how they canvassed the dancehalls and abortionists across the country looking for young meat? How they promise to make girls stars and then make them sluts?"

"I was lying when I said I didn't know what you were talking about before. But now I can say it and mean it."

He started to talk again but Scotti suddenly shook his head and coughed.

He looked around and a girl was standing in the doorway. She was one of those brown-eyed, blonde Sicilian girls who carried the sun with her wherever she went. She wore a blue quilted housecoat and in her hands she carried a tray full of food.

"This is my wife, Florence," Scotti said. "Detective Milazzo just dropped in to say hello."

She nodded and smiled and put the tray down.

"Do you like Italian coffee, Detective Milazzo?"

"Don't bother for me, honest."

"It's no bother. Would you like brandy with it?"

"Go ahead," Scotti said. "We have the best in liquor. My father-in-law owns a liquor store."

He looked at the spread. All neatly laid out. The china and the silver shone like the girl's eyes.

"And what kind of cake would you like, Detective?" she asked.

"Flo, he can help himself."

"Oh." The girl straightened up and smiled. "That's to let me know I'm supposed to leave."

"Right," Scotti said.

"Well, good night, Detective Milazzo."

He stood up and said good night.

"Excuse me a minute, Milazzo," Scotti said. "I'll be right back."

Scotti went to his wife and put his arm around her. For the first time he realized the girl was pregnant.

He watched them go out into the hall and then he sat down. The pink paper napkins had Flo and Ted printed in the corner. The cakes, the smell of good coffee and the sound of Scotti walking his wife up the stairs to say good night. That was the way some cops lived.

But not him. He lived in a hole like an animal. He was afraid to marry on a cop's crummy salary. He had stalled so long Gina finally took up with Rocky, and then he used that as an excuse.

And who was he to pass judgment on Gina? He wanted her to love him and be true to him and he never even had the courage to tell her how he felt.

All the wasted years when he could have had a home like this, a couple of kids and Gina.

And now it was too late. Scotti didn't know anything about the syndicate and he had to crack it by six—that is, if he lived until six. He remembered the chase down the street and being followed by a cab. At six they might be slipping what was left of him into the same meat wagon that had picked up Tony Statella.

Scotti finally came back and sat down.

"I'm sorry, Milazzo, but I don't like to talk shop in front of my wife. She still has the crazy notion that being a detective is a dignified job."

"I understand, Scotti, but about this syndicate, Rocky has told you nothing and I say one exists. Either I'm lying or Rocky's lying. The way I figure it Rocky is so crooked he can't even be an honest stool pigeon. He's playing you for a sucker."

"Yeah." The cold film was over Scotti's eyes again. "While I walked my wife upstairs I came to the same idea."

"What are you going to do about it?"

"Soon as you leave I'm going to dress and go downtown. Imagine—on Christmas. My wife will hate it. Then I'm going to wring Rocky like a dirty dishrag."

"It won't do any good. He'll sing a song about how I

cooked it up because I hate him."

"If he has anything to say I'll get it out of him."

From the look in Scotti's eyes he knew the guy meant business. But that would take too long. It would be too late to help Pete Rossi.

"Scotti, let me have him."

"Listen, Milazzo. I don't love the guy. To stand near him gives me the creeps. But he's my baby. I worked to get that cellar setup. I ran from office to office like a messenger boy. I crawled to get it okayed by the boys on top. Six months I waited until it started to pay off. Now it's become our main pipeline. You'd be surprised at the pinches that come out of that joint. Rocky gives me information from smuggled furs to ungraded beef. Do you think I'm going to throw all that away so you can get yourself some revenge?"

"It's more than me, Scotti. I want to see a good kid get a break."

"Gina Rossi's brother?"

"That's right."

"Some good kid. He blew a guy's brains out."

"I know the kid. We were like one family. He's a younger brother to me. How would you feel about your younger brother?"

"If he killed a guy?" Scotti thought and then shrugged. "I'd still have to arrest him."

"But Tony Statella deserved to die."

"That's not for me to decide. I'm just a cop. An instrument like a hammer to drive nails, or a vacuum cleaner for dirty rugs. I'm not supposed to have feelings or ideas. I just do a job."

The guy was right—but to come so close. He couldn't give up now.

"Look, Scotti, I'm going to level with you. I hate Rocky and I have plenty of reasons. Given half an alibi I'd have killed him this morning. I was out to frame him. But a couple of hours ago a miracle happened. I saw things clearer. It's not just hate. I'm a cop again. With one telephone call I can get enough information for the district attorney to break the filthiest combination that ever polluted the country. With the same call I get Pete Rossi a break. And me, I get another chance at life and my job. All that for one telephone call—if you give me Rocky."

"That's some miracle," Scotti said sadly. "It would be nice if there was room in it for me."

He smiled at that. It was funny. Now that the hate was in its place he could think so clearly.

"Look, Scotti, if Rocky were to die who would get the restaurant?"

Scotti thought a moment.

"I think he's got a younger brother."

"Do you know him?"

"Just to see him."

"Well, the brothers don't like each other—and they have good reasons. They're both rats. Paul has worked for me. Rocky works for you. Let's change."

"Swapping stoolies," Scotti smiled. "It doesn't make much sense."

"Why not? Whether you sweat Rocky or I sweat him when this syndicate thing breaks, the finger will be on Rocky. And you know how long he'll last."

"That's true," Scotti said. "No matter how you take care of them a stoolie's life is quick."

"Well, I'll give you a slightly used stoolie for a practically dead one. And your cellar setup is saved because brother Paul will move right in and take over. What do you say, Scotti?"

"When you put it that way what can I say?"

"Then it's a deal?"

Scotti nodded and they got up and shook hands.

In the small hall they wished each other a Merry Christmas and then Scotti gave him that boyish smile again.

"Miracle-man Milazzo. I always heard the talk about you. Well, they were right. You're the smartest cop I ever met."

"Don't kid yourself, Scotti." He looked over the guy's shoulder into the neat, sweet little house. "You're a hell of a lot smarter than I am."

He got into the car and Whiteman asked the usual question.

"Where to now?"

"Back to the city."

"And then?"

He would still play it close and careful.

"I'll tell you when we get there."

"Okay, Vince."

Back on the highway his partner started talking again.

"Since you told me they're out to kill you, I know why you've been acting so rough all evening. You're wondering right now if I'm the guy elected to deliver the bullet."

He didn't answer.

"I don't blame you, Vince. That's the way I'd feel. And that's the hell of it. You work with a guy for a year. You eat, walk, talk and spend more time with him than you do with your wife. Yet when the chips are down you got to watch him like a card sharp because he may be the guy who's out to get you. And the cop above? He may be square. He may be crooked. You never know. The cops below have a hundred reasons for selling you out. A smart cop doesn't trust anyone. That's why he's the loneliest guy in the world."

Even while his partner talked he wondered about Scotti. The guy seemed sincere. But right after he left the house Scotti might have gone to the phone and told the killer he was on his way back to Rocky.

"You know," Whiteman was still talking. "I once explained it to the wife. A cop is like a missionary fighting through a jungle. The jungle is full of animals and bugs and snakes and when the missionary gets through do the natives like him? Hell, no! They're thinking how good he'd taste in a stew. To me that's what a cop is like. Right, Vince?"

"A cop is an instrument—a hammer, a vacuum cleaner. He's got a job and he does it."

"Ha!" Whiteman said. "That's the crap. Once a day a cop straps on his gun and goes into the jungle to uphold the law. And what's the law? A lot of words put in a lot of books by a lot of lawyers. Even the guys who wrote the law can't agree on it. Even the boys in the Supreme Court are always arguing. Yet that's what a cop is supposed to uphold."

He wondered if Whiteman was trying to soften him up so he'd drop his guard.

"Once a day a cop straps on his gun," Whiteman said. "But with the gun he takes his heart or whatever you want to call it. The thing that tells him when to snap the cuffs on a guy's wrists or when to turn the other way."

Whiteman thought a moment, and then went on.

"A doctor decides important things; a wrong guess could kill someone. With a cop it's the same. Every day he's out in the jungle he's got to decide how to use the law. The wrong pinch can turn a frightened kid into a killer. Once I told a hysterical woman to go back home and not worry. She went back and when she opened the door her crazy husband shot her in the head. I was sick for weeks because I felt I killed her. But that's a cop's life. Those are the things he works out by himself every day."

Whiteman slowed the car down to make the overpass to the Triboro Bridge. Then he started talking again.

"At least a doctor gets respect. But a cop? Last week while off duty I saw a bunch of kids piling into a car. They were wearing evening clothes and they were well tanked. I could see a bent light pole, a smashed car and blood all over the nice clothes, so I made them take a cab. As they pulled away one of the dames called me a nosy flatfoot."

Whiteman laughed.

"And two days ago some kids on a roof dropped a bag of garbage on a cop. The whole neighborhood thought it was a big joke. What are you going to do?"

Whiteman shook his head sadly.

"No one gives us respect. We don't make money. We never know who's going to try and kill us. Yet each day we strap on a gun and go into the jungle to hold up the law. The thing I want to know, Vince, is why the hell do we do it?"

"That," he told his partner, "is one question I'll never be able to answer."

When they got back into town he told Whiteman to drive to Rocky's.

"You're crazy," Whiteman said. "That's one place they're sure to cover."

"I have to go there to make a telephone call."

"With all the telephones in this city? Are you kidding?"

"Besides, I'm hungry. I could go a plate of spaghetti."

"That makes sense." Whiteman said. "But does it have to be Rocky's joint?"

"Yeah."

"Then count me out. I saw the guy's menu. I'm no cheapskate, Vince, but last week I raised hell because the wife spent six dollars on a girdle. Now she's checking real close trying to find something to get back at me with."

"Okay, Whiteman, lend me another ten and I'll take you."

"What the hell," Whiteman laughed. "It's Christmas. I'll blow you to a plate of spaghetti and a glass of water."

He looked the ugly guy over and then shrugged. If Whiteman was on the level he'd be a good guy to have around. If not, what was one more gun in a crowd of guns?

When they got to Rocky's they parked right in front of the place and they looked the street over. It seemed safe. But he had that soft feeling behind the knees and he was sweating again.

"I'll go first and check." Whiteman said.

His partner got out, studied the street and then the stairs to the cellar. Finally Whiteman nodded.

He got out of the car, straightened his coat and slowly went down the stairs. Nobody was going to see how scared he was. Whiteman opened the door and they walked in.

Waiting in the hall was the same hat-check girl. She was wearing a low-cut blouse and she had enough blue on her eyes and enough red on her lips to camouflage a battle-ship.

"Hello, Mary Herchiemer," he said as he slipped off his coat.

She acted like she was busy with the hangers.

"I see you're still working here."

"Yes," she was angry. "They told me I had to stay in town for further questioning."

"You don't have to work here."

"Listen." She pointed at him. "You asked me questions this morning that you weren't supposed to. I know because my lawyer told me."

"Got a good lawyer, Mary?"

"The best, Mr. Detective, and from now on all I'll say to you is no comment."

"Yeah. He sounds like a good lawyer, Mary. And while

he's telling you what to say to the judge and jury let him tell you what to say to God."

He left the girl and started for the dining room.

"Remember your phone call," Whiteman said. "The booths are over there."

"Later on," he answered. "I still don't know who I'm going to call."

The headwaiter came bouncing over in his monkey suit and a big smile. When he got a better look at them the bounce left his walk and the smile left his face.

"You boys want to see the boss?"

"No. Just a plate of spaghetti."

"One plate for the two of you?" the headwaiter asked.

Then he led them all the way to a small table in the back. On one side the kitchen door swung open. And from the door on the other side he could smell the lavender disinfectant they used in the rest rooms.

"Some table," Whiteman said.

But he was satisfied. Sitting there with his back to the wall he could check all entrances without any trouble.

He looked at his watch. It was twelve-thirty.

He had five and a half hours in which to do the impossible.

It was late for him, but still early for Rocky's place.

An after-hour joint picked up its main business around three in the morning, when all the legit places closed. Then the guys who hated to go home, the entertainers who finished entertaining, and the scum, all gathered to drink and cut up and beat hell out of the Ten Commandments.

But even though it was early for an after-hour joint, Rocky's place was plenty full. The only lights were small lamps on the tables and all they showed was how much smoke there was in the air.

The thick carpet on the floor held the noise down and

the customers kept their voices low. All except the gang closest to him.

They had pulled four tables together and were laughing and talking and singing. He leaned over to see who was at the head of the table. By the rubbery face and rolling eyes he recognized Sammy Ray, the television comedian. From the way his friends laughed at everything Ray said it was easy to tell who was picking up the tab that night.

"You notice," Whiteman said, "how the waiters pass us by."

"Maybe they're busy."

"No. They're trying to make us feel cheap. Everybody loves to beat on a cop."

They waited and no one came. It was true. The waiters were giving them the freeze.

Whiteman waved his hand and the headwaiter came to the table.

"How about a little service?" Whiteman asked.

"That's what you're getting."

"You mean," Whiteman smiled, "as little as possible?"

The headwaiter shrugged.

Then he heard the dull crack as Whiteman's shoe hit the guy's shin. The headwaiter went down to grab the painful spot.

"What's that for?" he whined.

"I take it from taxpayers," Whiteman said softly. "But not from apes like you. Bring us two plates of spaghetti and a couple of beers."

"Yes, sir." The guy straightened up.

"And I'm holding you responsible," Whiteman said. "If anybody in the kitchen spits in that spaghetti I'll crack your skull."

"Oh, I won't let them, sir."

The guy took off in a hurry.

"When you're a cop long enough," Whiteman said,

"you get to know what they think before they think it."

"I know what you mean," he said. "That's exactly what I'm betting my life on."

The service began to click. A couple of waiters spread out the silver. Another brought a pitcher of ice water. Then the bread sticks, the butter, cheese, beer and two plates of spaghetti came. But he was more interested in looking around.

There were the society playboys, the out-of-town buyers with the over-friendly models; and in one corner he saw Luther Kennedy, the Broadway musical director.

The wavy-haired blond boy sitting next to Luther he didn't know. But he remembered some of the stories going around town, and from the way the two guys were sitting real close to each other it seemed Luther was out to prove the stories were true.

At another table he saw Moe Fields, the fight manager, attacking a steak. Alongside was his pug, King Swab. Swab the slob, the papers called him. They said he became a fighter because he loved to skip rope. His last thirty fights were supposed to have been bought. But it wasn't bothering the King. He was busy letting the two girls at the table feel the muscles on his arms and his back.

Then he saw someone at another table. Someone more interesting. It was Harry Farmen, the gambler. Farmen was a tough cookie with a bad temper. He couldn't place the other four men at the table. Maybe some suckers Farmen was getting lined up for a take.

He was just about to decide on the gambler when he saw Big Frank Bellow at another table. Big Frank was an old time organization man who had been through the mill. He was supposed to be clean now, with a big trucking outfit, a fleet of cabs and a brewery. But the old-timers never really got out of it.

Frank was sitting at the table with a couple of stooges

and a beautiful girl. Her dress was one of those seven-hundred-dollar French originals. Her silver mink coat was half on the chair, half on the floor, and the diamonds around her fingers and wrists sparkled like Times Square at midnight. She looked very bored, and the only time she stopped picking her teeth was when she yawned.

Big Frank Bellow was his best bet.

"I'm going to place my call, Whiteman."

The booths were in back of the coat room. He went into the first one and memorized the number. Then he went into the second booth and called it.

He saw the hat-check girl coming to answer. He closed the door to his booth and waited.

"Hello," she said.

He made his voice real low so she wouldn't recognize it. "I want to talk to Frank Bellow."

"One moment."

He watched her leave the booth and talk to a waiter. In a few minutes Big Frank came into view. The way the guy stopped to check all around before he stepped into the phone booth showed he was an old-timer. So many of the boys got it in the back while answering a phone.

"Hello."

"This Big Frank?"

"Yeah."

"Nice John said to call."

"What's up?"

"Rocky Tosco is a stoolie for the cops."

"What!" It was so loud he heard it twice. Once over the phone and once through the wall of the booth.

"That's right, Big Frank. Nice John says pass the word. It's open season on rats. I got to make more calls."

He hung up and waited.

Big Frank came out and stood there rubbing his jaw. Then suddenly Big Frank hurried to his table.

The door of the phone booth was in the way so he swung it open to see better.

When Big Frank reached the table he said something that made the men jump. One got up so fast he bumped into a waiter.

But the beauty with the fancy clothes decided she wanted to stay, because she didn't get up. Big Frank kicked the leg of her chair so hard it spun around under her and she had to grab the table to keep from falling.

Big Frank and his boys were outside before the beauty grabbed her mink and followed.

Now it was going to happen.

Talk about jungle drums, or smoke signals, or even the telegraph. The underworld had its own system. The whispered word would go out. One told five. Five told twenty-five.

Like a ricocheting bullet the word would bounce around the city. And like a ricocheting bullet it would bounce just as hard and be just as dangerous.

Guys would remember a friend who was in Rocky's joint two nights before he was pinched, or a brother who used to eat at Rocky's regular but was now in the death-house.

Some of the hunches would be right, some of them wrong. But a rat was a rat. All hell would soon break loose.

He left the phone booth and went back to the table to wait.

A girl sitting near the comedian jumped up with a scream. She poked her hand down the front of her dress and dug around.

"I told you, Sammy," she moaned. "No more ice cubes."

"Let me help you." The comedian reached over and pushed a stalk of celery down the back of her dress.

"Ah, Sammy," the girl said.

She pulled the celery out and threw it on the table. Then she dug for the ice cube again.

"Shake it loose, kid," Sammy said.

The girl stepped away from the table and began to wiggle her shoulders. Soon all her parts were moving and Sammy Ray was banging on the table crying for more.

The girl crouched low for a slow juicy grind. She yipped like a Texas cowhand, flipped her dress over her face and squeezed out a bump. Then she sat down.

"Again! Again!" the comedian screamed.

He sighed sadly and turned to look at Whiteman.

"The guy's jerk happy."

"Blame his mother," Whiteman said. "She should have given him a ukulele to play with when he was a kid."

The Broadway director was holding the blond boy's hand. The two girls were now feeling the muscles on the prize fighter's legs and his manager was tearing into another steak.

More people came in, but no one he was waiting for. He looked at his watch.

It was almost two o'clock.

What was taking Frank Bellow so long? Maybe his plan had gone sour. Maybe using Nice John's name had been a mistake. He was wondering if he'd have to make another call when Suitcase Sulkin came into the restaurant. Suitcase was a smalltime ticket speculator and he seemed more nervous than ever as he hurried over to Moe Field's table.

The fight manager worked on his steak as Suitcase leaned close and whispered. The knife and fork slowed down and finally they stopped.

Then suddenly, with the knife and fork still in his hand, Moe Fields got up and crossed the restaurant to Farmen's table.

The tough gambler looked up and listened to the fight manager. Then Farmen jumped to his feet so fast the table tipped and things fell to the floor.

The restaurant grew quiet as people turned to look.

"Come on." Farmen was talking real loud. "Let's get out of this crummy joint."

The headwaiter went running over.

"Something wrong, sir?"

Farmen picked up a glass of wine and splashed the red stuff in the guy's face.

"That's for your boss." Farmen was talking loud enough for the whole place to hear. "Tell him I hate rats."

The crowd was stunned. The headwaiter just stood there with his mouth open as the wine ran down his shirt front.

Farmen and his four friends walked out of the place.

Moe Fields went back to his table and he suddenly realized he was still carrying the knife and fork. He threw them down on the table.

"Come on," he said to King Swab. "Let's blow."

"Why?" The fighter smiled at the two girls. "I like it here."

The manager leaned over and pushed the girls' hands off his fighter.

"You can get your rubdown in the gym. Come on."

"But I like it here."

The manager pointed to the door and the King got up like a trained bear and they both started out.

On the way to the door Moe Fields stopped at another table and there was some whispering. More people got up. They all left together.

That's the way it would be all over the city. In the bars, and the gyms, and the pool rooms, and all gambling joints.

The whispered word would be going from mouth to mouth. Minds would begin to click. Old wounds would open. Old hates would break out again. Guns would come from dark closets and under floor boards. Alone, or in twos and threes, men would be making plans to kill

Rocky because it was always open season on rats.

"Wonder what hit Farmen?" Whiteman asked. "Do you think he found a hair in his soup?"

"No." He watched his partner closely. "He just found out Rocky Tosco was a stoolie."

Whiteman started to laugh. He laughed so hard everything on the table jiggled.

"That explains a lot of things," he said between laughs.

The headwaiter finally came out of his daze. He hurried over to the office, knocked on the door and went in.

Rocky came out of the office. He was still calm and still smiling. He stood there holding his hands up in the air like a master of ceremonies stopping applause.

"Sorry, folks. We had a little disturbance. One of our guests lost a big bet or something."

The crowd relaxed and the conversation started buzzing again. Rocky went from table to table, talking, laughing, the perfect restaurateur.

"Either the guy doesn't know yet," Whiteman said, "or he has plenty of guts."

In a few minutes the joint was back to normal. Then Rocky came to their table.

"Milazzo," he asked quietly. "Did you make Farmen flip his lid?"

"In a way. I let the word out you were a part-time cop."

Not a twitch in the guy's face. He just rested his big heavy fists on the table.

"For that," Rocky said. "You die."

"So people keep telling me."

Rocky picked up his fists and turned to go.

"If you're going to call your friend Scotti you can save the phone fare."

Rocky came back to listen.

"I just swapped Scotti two old razor blades for you. From now on you're in my cage. You sing for me."

"That's what you think." Rocky banged his chest with his fist. "I talk to who I want. And to you I don't want. I got plenty of important friends, Milazzo, and you're in trouble."

"If you're thinking of the chief he's on my side. And if you're thinking of your pals in the syndicate they'll be the first to want to kill you."

"Nobody is killing me."

"No?" He turned and winked at his partner. "Friend Rocky stays close to his office. Tell him what word is going around the street."

"It's bad, Rocky," Whiteman said. "The boys at the station house have a pool on what hour you get it."

Rocky started to go again but he reached out and held the guy's arm.

"Rocky, you have a chance. There's one place bullets won't touch you. You'll be safe behind my police shield."

"So?"

"I want to know all about the syndicate."

"When pigs fly I'll tell you."

"Sooner than that, Rocky. I'm going now. But I got the car parked right outside. I'll wait thirty minutes. If you're not there by then, you're on your own. Come on, Whiteman."

They got up and left Rocky standing there. A couple of times he wanted to turn back to see how Rocky was taking the news but he knew Rocky would be watching to see if he was nervous, to see if it was all a bluff.

When he took his coat from the hat-check girl he threw half a buck on the counter.

"That's to help you pay for your shyster, Mary."

Then he followed his partner out.

"I'll go up first and see what's doing," Whiteman said. When Whiteman got to the top of the steps he looked around.

"Seems quiet, Vince."

He followed up and they both got into the car.

"I know what you're doing," Whiteman said. "You're trying to pressure him into talking. But Rocky is no ordinary pigeon. You can't expect him to crack in thirty minutes."

"I'd like to give him more time." He looked at the clock on the dashboard. It was going on three. "But in three hours I've got to break this wide open or the chief is going to break me—if there's enough left of me to break."

"But half an hour, Vince. That's not much time to crack a guy like Rocky. He's tough."

"Rocky? Yeah, he's tough. When he was a kid he was tough because he knew if anyone touched him his old man would come running out of the butcher shop with a knife. Then his older brother backed him up in his fights. Later on when he was in the Navy the uniform put the starch in his spine. In the stick-up game he depended on the LaSalle brothers. Then he got Detective Scotti to protect him. He always had someone to make him feel brave. Now for the first time in his life he has no one to turn to, no one to back him—except me. The pattern is set. Rocky Tosco can't stand alone. He'll come running."

"I hope so," Whiteman said.

"He's got to." He sounded sure, but inside he was wondering....

Ten minutes passed.

Ten empty wasted minutes. Then he saw something in a doorway.

He poked Whiteman with his elbow.

"Look across the street," he said. "Four houses down. In the door."

"Someone's there, all right." Whiteman said. "Don't stop me this time, Vince. I'm going over and check. Keep me covered."

Whiteman swung out of the car and started across the street.

The guy had guts. He didn't crouch or run. He stood up straight and walked right into it.

The shadow in the doorway didn't try to make a break as Whiteman came toward it. He could see Whiteman talking. Then his partner came back and got into the car laughing.

"It was a couple of kids mushing it up in the dark. I scared hell out of them."

"They scared hell out of me, too."

"Yeah," Whiteman said. "When the pressure is on, things get under your skin. Every time you see a shadow you swear it's a punk with a gun."

"The guy who chased me down the street was no shadow."

"Maybe not."

"Well, what about the cab that tailed us? Was that a shadow?"

"No," Whiteman admitted. "That was real."

Then they saw a familiar figure coming down the street. It was Handy Moore, one of Tony Statella's boys. He was walking fast and he took the stairs down to the cellar in a hurry.

"Could be more pressure," Whiteman said.

"Every bit helps."

"What will you do if Rocky doesn't break?"

"I won't even think about it."

Suddenly they heard the door bang open and excited voices came from the cellar. The first one up was Handy Moore. Right behind him was the headwaiter, waving his hands as he talked.

"I was fooled like everyone else. Do you think I knew he was a stoolie? This thing can ruin my reputation."

"I've heard," Whiteman said, "of rats leaving a sinking

ship. But what do they call things that leave a sinking rat?"

The restaurant door banged open again and someone else ran up the stairs.

"Hey, wait for me." It was one of the waiters. "I had to tell Jerry." He ran down the street after the others.

"Seven minutes to go," Whiteman said.

The door opened again and they heard someone else coming up the stairs, only this time it was slow. He could feel his collar grow wet as he waited.

It was Rocky, all right.

Rocky was coming up slowly, buttoning his overcoat and still smiling. He came to the car and Whiteman lowered the window.

"So you want information?" he asked as if the conversation had never stopped.

"That's right, Rocky."

"I've got a deal. I'll give you what you want. You give me three things."

"Let's have it."

"First. I don't get manhandled."

"All right, Rocky."

"Second. I'm a material witness and I don't want to be caged up in a cell."

"Check."

"And last. I want police protection as long as I'm in danger."

He thought that one over, then smiled.

"We'll protect you as if you were a taxpayer, Rocky."

He stepped out of the car and let Rocky in.

"Okay, Whiteman." He got back in and slammed the door. "The station house."

They drove three blocks, then suddenly Whiteman took a crazy turn, kicked off the siren and stepped on the gas.

"What's the matter?" he asked.

"A taxi is tailing us again."

"Shake it," he said. And once more he was sweating.

Only this time he wasn't alone. Rocky Tosco's forehead was covered with sweat too.

It was three-thirty-five.

Christmas morning.

The station house was full of puking drunks and bad-smelling bums. But he had never been so glad to get inside the thick walls of the old building.

"It was a mistake," some guy was telling the sergeant. "I got a blue car. And this was blue car. So I thought it was mine. That's why I got in."

"Do you always smash a window to get into your car?"

There was a little girl wrapped in a police coat, and a sad-looking cop was trying to keep her happy by making crazy shadows on the wall with his hands.

"Baby sitting?" Whiteman asked as they passed.

"She was roaming the streets," the cop said, "looking for Santa Claus. And I had to find her."

As they pushed through toward the stairs a big-mouthed, big-hipped babe grabbed Whiteman's arm.

"Do you have any drag here?" she asked.

"I'm just in charge of the loose floor boards, lady." Whiteman pulled away and they kept on going.

"Peace on earth." The dame screamed above the rest of the noise. "You'd think this is one day they'd let us girls alone."

Upstairs it was just as busy.

One detective was turning a mean knife around in his hand and the kid in front of the desk shrugged.

"I use it to open beer cans."

"Yeah," the detective said. "But that guy was no beer can."

They went to the homicide room and that was filled

too. A crying girl, a sulking fellow and a tired detective.

"Let's try the chief's office."

The small room was empty. One at a time they squeezed by the filing cabinets near the door and he motioned Rocky to the chair behind the desk.

Rocky hung his fancy coat on the rack. Then he sat down and rocked the chief's chair back and forth testing it, with a smile on his face.

Behind Rocky was a window. It looked out on the side of an old tenement house. It was a crazy idea. But he couldn't forget the cab that followed them.

"Whiteman, will you pull the blind?"

He waited until his partner got the creaky shade down, and then he looked at his watch.

Two hours to go.

That didn't leave much time to work on Rocky. He would use butter. Flattery was sometimes the best way to grease a punk's tongue.

"That was smart the way you tricked Scotti."

"Scotti's a jerk," Rocky went back in the chair. "He trusted me. So I threw the guy a few crumbs and behind his back I milked the syndicate."

"If I know you, Rocky, you were probably one of the top men."

"In a way you could say I started it. One night I went around to the club and complained to Tony. The dame he sent to check coats was such a bag she made my customers lose their appetites. Tony said all us restaurant guys wanted pretty hat chicks."

Rocky shrugged.

"I said sure a pretty slut was good for business and everyone around the table agreed. That's how I started the idea."

"Who was around the table?"

"Tony, Frank Betti—" Rocky rubbed his heavy jaw and

thought. "Your Uncle Ralph was there, and Handy Moore. But that had nothing to do with the syndicate. That was just how I started the idea."

"It was a good idea. Tell me more about it."

Rocky was enjoying himself. "If a bar owner has a dame sitting near the door with her legs crossed, every wolf who passes is going to spot the bait and stop for a drink. Sometimes the barkeep uses a local bag. But the trick is to keep changing the bait. A new face, a new set of legs and the same suckers keep coming back. Every bar in the country could use a fresh bag every week."

"A girl-of-the-week club," he said.

"Yeah." Rocky threw his heavy head back and laughed. "But that was only one gimmick. We kicked the idea around all night and got plenty of angles. Then I went home and forgot it.

"But not friend Tony." From the way he said it you could see Rocky thought friend Tony was smarter than Einstein. "In two weeks Tony asks me if I want to buy in on a black book. Right away I ask where are we going to get the meat to throw to the suckers, and Tony tells me how my idea has grown.

"You see." Rocky came forward in the chair. He was all excited and moving his big hands as he explained. "Hundreds of dames come to the city to be stars or models. So the syndicate opened singing and dancing schools and a model agency."

"Smart," he said. "Then you didn't have to look for the girls. They looked for you."

"That was the angle." Rocky smiled proudly. "When the dames came we interviewed them. Found out how fast they could be pushed. Some were ready to go all the way right from the start.

"With the others," Rocky dropped a heavy lid over his eye in a slow wink. "We took it easy. First we fed them a couple of jobs posing for sexy covers on cheap magazines and took their money away for lessons. When we finally got a dish broke and hungry we talked her into posing for a strip set. After that we talked to her about being a call girl. It wasn't always easy, but sooner or later we broke their backs."

Rocky had himself a good laugh. Then he went on talking.

"A starving kid finds it hard to look away from a five-hundred-dollar bill even if it is her first time. Then we had her on the hook. When the five hundred dollar boys were finished using her we threw her to the fifty and twenty-dollar crowd. The girl had to circulate more, but it was still money.

"That's when I gave friend Tony another gimmick." Rocky threw out his big chest and tapped it proudly. "When a dame was used up in New York, why not peddle her in another town. So we built a list of stops across the country. Some worked the joints as bar girls and some as chorus girls. The better built ones were strippers. Others just sat in their rooms until the phone rang. When the customers got tired using them we shipped the meat on to a new spot. And we always got our cut two ways. The joints paid us a fee for supplying the dame and the dame kicked in because we supplied them with joints."

He wanted to open a window and let some fresh air in but he just nodded.

"Pretty slick. Go on, Rocky."

"Hell, that wasn't all. Tony's department was a squad of shake-down specialists. They blackmailed the rich customers and if a dame got a break like becoming a big-time star or getting married we milked her too."

"And what was your department, Rocky?"

"Well, that was our stock in trade. The more dames we started on their way the more money we made. So besides my after-hour place I had a specialty. A real good-looking but stubborn kid Tony would steer my way. I was death on them. They can't resist me." Rocky brushed his lapel and smiled. "I showed them a good time and when they trusted me I talked them into my apartment. A couple of drinks and they were mine."

"What did you do? Use knockout drops?"

"Not always," Rocky protested. "Sometimes it was just charm. Sometimes—" He felt his muscle and winked. "I'm a pretty strong guy, Vince. Then," he shrugged, "when I was finished with the dish I tossed her out. Tony would go to see her and tell her now that it was started she had nothing to lose. You'd be surprised how many kids I started that way."

He saw Whiteman's hands double up into a fist. He caught his partner's eye and shook his head. This was no time for satisfaction.

"Yeah, Rocky," he said. "You guys had it down to a system. But who was on top? Who was the Number One?"

"That I don't know, Vince."

"What?" He found himself shouting. "Are you on the level?"

"Honest, Vince. I tried to find out but Tony wouldn't even give me a hint. He wouldn't even let me see the black book. It's in a cigar box in a safe. That's all he'd tell me."

He felt like kicking a hole in the filing cabinet or putting his fist through the wall.

"If you can't tell me that what good are you?"

"I can give you everything else. Look." Rocky took a brown notebook from his pocket. "Scotti never wanted me to try and remember things or try and decide what was important. I was supposed to write everything I heard the minute I got the chance. Well, I did. One notebook was for Scotti. But the stuff on the syndicate I kept in this."

He reached over and took the notebook.

"It's got everything, Vince—the girls, the customers, the joints—and all the guys in the syndicate."

He looked into the book. It read like a diary—dates, names, and what was said, all neatly printed.

Even as he double-crossed Scotti, Rocky was storing away for the day he'd double-cross the syndicate. The guy was a born rat.

But the important things were still missing. Who was the Number One, and where was the black book? Somewhere in Rocky's notebook he might find a clue.

He was going through the pages when someone outside called.

"Milazzo, there's a guy downstairs to see you."

"Whiteman," he said, and didn't even look up. "Find out what it is."

He stopped long enough to let Whiteman get by, and then he started reading the notebook again.

There was a list of girls Rocky started on their way. A list of people being blackmailed. Everything a district attorney could want—except two things.

He looked at his watch.

One hour and fifteen minutes to go. The sweat was making his collar stick to his neck.

Then Whiteman came back.

"Who was it?" he asked.

"This is going to make you feel stupid, Vince. It was Money-mad Minetta with a hot tip. He's been after us all over town."

"You mean he's the guy who chased me down the street?"

"Yeah," Whiteman laughed. "And a couple of times in a cab too."

So he'd been running from a stoolie all night. A stoolie

who just wanted to give him a tip.

When you're in trouble every shadow looks like a punk with a gun. But that wet soft feeling was too fresh in his mind.

"What did Money-mad have to tell me?"

Whiteman grinned.

"That you were going to be killed by morning if you didn't lay off the syndicate."

"Fresh stuff," he said in disgust. Then suddenly he looked up from the notebook. "Where did Money-mad get his news?"

"That's the first thing I asked him. Finally I persuaded him to talk. Get set for a shock. Someone gave Money-mad a hundred bucks to pass the phony word. The someone was your Uncle Ralph."

His uncle. His rotten uncle.

Sure. Ralph was calm until he said he was out to smash the syndicate. Then his Uncle Ralph got the panic. First he tried to buy him off with fifty grand. Then he tried to scare him off by saying he would get killed.

Well, there it was. He took the piece of memo paper from his pocket and dialed Bell.

"Hello." The guy's voice was full of sleep.

"Milazzo calling. Come on down, Bell. And bring your overworked staff. I have the stuff I promised."

"You have!" The sleep left Bell's voice.

"I'll give you a thousand people to subpoena. You'll have more witnesses than a shyster's got tricks."

"And the black book?"

"The black book." He looked at Rocky and smiled. "You'll find it in a cigar box inside the safe of the Supreme Leather Works Inc. The president, Mr. Ralph Milazzo, is the head of the syndicate. But you better move fast. He knows the heat is on."

"I'll be there," he said. "Give me half an hour."

He looked at his watch. He had fifty minutes left.

"A half-hour will just about make it."

As he hung up he reached for the phone book. He looked for a number and called again.

"Hello, Gina? ... This is Vincent talking ... Is your kid brother around? Good ... Pack him in a taxi and get him down to the station fast ... Yes, Gina. I swung a deal. Your brother will get a break ... Don't thank me now, Gina." He looked at his watch. "Just get him here in fifteen minutes.

"And Gina." He started to say something, and then he looked at the men in the office. He had waited so long to say it he could wait a few minutes more. "I'll tell you when you get here, Gina."

He hung up the phone.

"Was that Gina Rossi?" Rocky asked.

"Yeah."

"That's one dame I can't stand."

"Why? Was she too smart for you?"

"Don't worry," Rocky said. "I got even with her. When she brushed me off I went around the neighborhood and told everybody what good game she was. I also told them to stay away from her because she gave me a bad dose of crud." Rocky laughed uproariously. Finally he simmered down. "Maybe they didn't swallow all of it. But they swallowed enough to ruin Gina's reputation."

And he had been one of the fools to believe it. Well, he'd spend the rest of his life making it up to her.

"Okay, Rocky." He kept his voice nice and even. "You can go home now and ruin some more girls."

Rocky put on his coat and stood there waiting.

"I figure I'll need six detectives for protection," Rocky finally said.

"Six detectives?"

"Sure. Two on. Four off. Eight-hour shifts around the

clock."

"You're nuts."

Rocky was still smiling but his fingers played with a coat button.

"I'm your star witness, Vince."

"No, you're not, Rocky." He held the brown notebook up. "Here are all the witnesses I'll need."

"How many detectives you going to assign to protect me?"

"None."

Rocky's fingers twitched and the button came loose from the coat.

"You promised, Vince."

"That's right." He pulled change from his pocket and picked out a dime. "Protection just like a taxpayer." He tossed the dime on the desk. "If you're in trouble dial the operator and ask for a policeman."

The button dropped from Rocky's fingers and rolled across the floor.

"They'll kill me." The guy was still smiling. "Frank Betti, Handy Moore, Farmen, Moe Fields, Nice John's goons. If you send me out into the street it's like killing me yourself."

"I spread the word on you, Rocky, to force you to talk. But if I didn't someone else would have figured you out. Tomorrow or the next day you would have gotten it. A stoolie's life is quick. Now beat it. The place is beginning to stink."

Rocky sat down on the chief's chair.

"I'm not going."

He looked at his partner and Whiteman nodded.

Rocky was a head taller and thirty pounds heavier, but Whiteman grabbed his shoulder and pulled Rocky out of the seat.

"Don't you see, Vince?" Rocky was still smiling. "Don't

you understand? They'll kill me."

Whiteman took a handful of coat collar and steered Rocky toward the door. The guy was a soft hulk of fear, but the cocky smile was still pasted on his face. It looked like a ten-cent Halloween mask.

Suddenly Rocky started screaming.

"They'll kill me!" His heavy hand grabbed one of the handles of the filing cabinet and he hung on while Whiteman tried to shake him loose. "Don't you understand? They'll kill me."

Finally Whiteman got him outside.

He heard the guy crying all the way down the stairs, and then it got quiet.

He walked over to the window and let the shade go up with a snap.

Cold white winter light came in. There was fresh snow on the window ledge outside and the church bells were ringing. It was Christmas morning.

THE END

Louis Malley was born and raised in New York City. He lived in Harlem, the Bronx and Little Italy neighborhoods, where he got involved with the gangs. He eventually left the streets to take on various jobs including writing political slogans and working as a bouncer at a 125th Street bar. Malley wrote four gritty novels set in the world he grew up in, beginning with the hardback publication of *Horns for the Devil* in 1951, which received the French Grand Prix de Littérature Policièrein award in 1953. His last novel, *The Love Mill*, appeared in 1961. According to a newspaper report, Malley was shot and killed in 1962 at age 40.

Black Gat Books

Black Gat Books is a new line of mass market paperbacks introduced in 2015 by Stark House Press. New titles appear every three months, featuring the best in crime fiction reprints. Each book is sized to 4.25" x 7", just like they used to be. Collect them all! $9.99 each.

1 Haven for the Damned
by Harry Whittington
978-1-933586-75-5

2 Eddie's World
by Charlie Stella
978-1-933586-76-2

3 Stranger at Home
by Leigh Brackett writing as George Sanders
978-1-933586-78-6

4 The Persian Cat
by John Flagg
978-1933586-90-8

5 Only the Wicked
by Gary Phillips
978-1-933586-93-9

6 Felony Tank
by Malcolm Braly
978-1-933586-91-5

7 The Girl on the Bestseller List
by Vin Packer
978-1-933586-98-4

8 She Got What She Wanted
by Orrie Hitt
978-1-944520-04-5

9 The Woman on he Roof
by Helen Nielsen
978-1-944520-13-7

10 Angel's Flight
by Lou Cameron
978-1-944520-18-2

11 The Affair of Lady Westcott's Lost Ruby / The Case of the Unseen Assassin
by Gary Lovisi
978-1-944520-22-9

12 The Last Notch
by Arnold Hano
978-1-944520-31-1

13 Never Say No to a Killer
by Clifton Adams
978-1-944520-36-6

14 The Men from the Boys
by Ed Lacy
978-1-944520-46-5

15 Frenzy of Evil
by Henry Kane
978-1-944520-53-3

16 You'll Get Yours
by William Ard
978-1-944520-54-0

17 End of the Line
by Dolores & Bert Hitchens
978-1-944520-57-1

18 Frantic
by Noël Calef
978-1-944520-66-3

19 The Hoods Take Over
by Ovid Demaris
978-10944520-73-1

20 Madball by Fredric Brown
978-1-944520-74-8

Stark House Press

1315 H Street, Eureka, CA 95501 707-498-3135
griffinskye3@sbcglobal.net www.starkhousepress.com

Available from your local bookstore or direct from the publisher.